Any Way You Want It
The Moments in Maplesville Series

Farrah Rochon

Nicobar Press

Special thanks to
my aunt, Catherine Gray, for providing the
scenery featured on this cover.

Any Way You Want It
The Moments in Maplesville Series

Chapter One

Rain pelted the yellow rain slicker Nyree Grant draped over her head as she jogged to the passenger side of her Mazda CX-5. She lifted a cardboard box full of generic brown plastic bottles and cradled it against her ribcage.

Cursing the thunderstorm that sprouted out of nowhere on her drive over, Nyree had even more choice words for the nasty weather that had delayed the shipment of custom containers she planned to use for her homemade hair products. It totally screwed up her surprise. She'd intended to wow her friends with her new, professional packaging.

"It's what's inside that counts," Nyree murmured as she climbed the wooden steps leading up to her friend Reesa Patterson's hair salon. She balanced the carton of shampoo, leave-in conditioner and hair-curling pudding on her hip as she fiddled with the rain-slicked door handle.

Ugh. She forgot about this rickety thing; it was always getting stuck.

"Open up," Nyree called, hefting the box

higher on her hip.

Seconds later, the door opened and something resembling Cousin Itt from *The Addam's Family* appeared.

Nyree yelped.

Cheyenne Bradley flipped the hair from her face. "The post office went up on stamps again, nobody's sending you an engraved invitation to come inside."

"Smart ass," Nyree said as she shouldered past Cheyenne and made her way into the small twenty-by-twenty converted garage Reesa rented in their tiny hometown of St. Pierre, Louisiana. Reesa had taken over where Nyree's aunt, Hazel, had left off. For years her aunt had been the only hairdresser in St. Pierre. She'd trained Reesa and left her with a loyal clientele.

But, in Nyree's opinion, her friend had outgrown this place a long time ago. And now that Reesa had competition from a bigger salon that had moved into the town's only strip mall, she needed to step up her game.

"Please, tell me you brought the jojoba hot oil treatment?" Reesa asked from behind the chair where she'd gone back to sewing long locks of frosted blonde synthetic hair onto Cheyenne's head.

"I have that one, but I also brought another that I've been working on." Nyree tossed a sealed jar into Cheyenne's lap. "It's a combination of whipped coconut oil and vegetable glycerin."

She began stacking the jars and bottles on the tiny shelf at the rear of Reesa's shop. So far, this was the only place where people could buy her skin and hair care creations, but soon enough she'd have an entire room to showcase the myriad products she'd spent the past two years developing. Just the thought of it sent a tremor of anxious excitement skittering along Nyree's skin.

She was so close.

It had taken some heavy campaigning, but if there was one thing Nyree could do, it was talk a good game. She'd finally convinced her three friends that banding together to open an all-inclusive salon and spa was the most spectacular idea in the history of spectacular ideas.

Now, she just needed to make it happen within the next two months.

And she would. She *had* to. Reesa, Cheyenne, and Amara were counting on her to make this happen, and disappointing her girls was out of the question.

This concept was the first of its kind in this area. Right now, a person had to travel for more than an hour—all the way to New Orleans—to find a one-stop shop for all beauty and pampering needs on the scale of what Nyree envisioned for Any Way You Want It, their soon-to-be salon and spa. Between the four of them, they had everything they needed.

Reesa had been styling hair well before she was licensed by the state to do it. The same was true for Cheyenne and her massages, though it was unlikely the guys on the basketball team back in high school cared whether or not Cheyenne's rubdowns were sanctioned by the state.

Amara Doucet, the makeup artist in their quartet, could identify the exact color and brand of lipstick a woman wore within seconds of meeting her. She was so eerily good at it that people told her she could take her makeup-guessing-game act on the road.

Nyree was the only member of their foursome who didn't do anything hands-on. She used her talents behind the scenes, taking advantage of her chemistry degree to develop a line of organic hair and skincare products. She'd worked tirelessly over the past two years, perfecting her recipes in her spare time, making sure her products could stand up next to anything on the market today.

Pride welled within Nyree's chest.

She'd never held a shred of doubt that she would make this dream a reality, but even she hadn't imagined that it would happen quite this quickly.

It hasn't happened yet.

But it would. Despite the doubts that annoying voice tried to plant into her brain.

Of course, it would have been easier to ignore that voice a couple of days ago, back when she didn't have to worry about finding a contractor to complete the renovations on the late nineteenth-century Greek Revival she'd just purchased to house their new venture. Using the bulk of the money her aunt Hazel left her for the down payment, Nyree hadn't considered saving any to pay a contractor. Why would she when her two older brothers owned their own construction business and had offered to do the work for free?

She should have known better.

How many times over the past twenty-four years had her brothers, Desmond and Lance, come up with excuses for why they couldn't fulfill promises they'd made? Nyree had yet to forgive Lance for reneging on his promise to drive her to the LSU Math Competition back in her junior year of high school. She was the only member of the St. Pierre Math-o-holics who didn't get to compete.

But this was more important than a high school math contest. This was her dream. It was her three best friends' dreams, too. And, once again, her brothers were letting her down.

Okay, fine. So maybe she *had* moved up the timetable for construction by a couple of months, but it wasn't as if she hadn't given Desmond a head's up. She'd called him as soon as she'd left the lawyer's office with her real estate agent, letting him know that she'd convinced the Whitmer family to close on the sale early. He'd just mentioned during Sunday dinner that he and Lance had finished the big job they'd been working on, and had some time off before the next one would start.

It wasn't that Desmond and Lance *couldn't* help her, it's that they wouldn't. And she knew changing the start date on them wasn't that big of an issue. Nyree had seen them adjust their work schedules for clients in the past.

No, it's because her brothers didn't take her "little beauty products business" seriously.

And that's what hurt the most.

They thought she was playing around, wasting her time with this little hobby of hers.

Nyree was done listening to them criticize what she considered her most important achievement. She didn't need those two. In fact, she wouldn't accept their help now even if they dropped everything to work on The Whitmer House.

Of course, that meant she was now stuck having to search for a new contractor. Someone who wouldn't push the work aside because they had more important clients to tend to. Someone who wouldn't charge her an arm and a leg. Someone who would be able to complete the work in less than two months.

Nyree fought the panic attack that was so very close to taking her down.

She didn't have time to panic. Her nervous breakdown would have to wait until after Any Way You Want It's grand opening in a couple of months.

Besides, today was a day to celebrate all of her hard work. She'd resisted telling the girls about closing early on the house, on the slim chance that she wouldn't be able to make it happen. Even though in her mind it was never a question. Once Nyree decided that the grand opening for Any Way You Want It would take place on what would have been her Aunt Hazel's 50th birthday, there was nothing that would stop it from happening. They were opening their doors on April 4th, even if she had to do all the work herself.

Feigning nonchalance, Nyree plopped into the shop's remaining vinyl salon chair. The towel draped over the left armrest covered a huge swath of duct tape that Reesa had to replace every few weeks. Three state-of-the-art chairs, with padded seats and removable headrests, were in route from a warehouse in California. There would be no duct tape-covered anything in their new digs.

Because it was the middle of the day, the only other person in the shop was one of Reesa's senior-citizen regulars who came in for a weekly wash and roller set. She sat under the domed hair dryer, lost in an edition of *Us Weekly*.

"So, what's good?" Nyree asked, grabbing a red sucker from the bowl of hard candy on the shelf. It was an ode to Aunt Hazel, who used to keep candy readily available for patrons in her salon.

"I should be asking you that," Reesa said. "How are things going with the Whitmer House?"

"Oh, I'd say they're going okay." Nyree slipped a hand in her pocket and pulled out a single key hanging from a red and white Chauvin Realty key ring.

Reesa gasped. "Is that the key to the house?"

"*What?*" Cheyenne lifted the hair from her face again. "How did you convince them to give you the key already?"

A massive smile broke out across Nyree's face. "Because I closed on the house yesterday," she said.

The three of them erupted in squeals, then simultaneously apologized to the customer who jumped from under the hair dryer, her eyes widened in shock.

"I'm so sorry, Mrs. Holston," Reesa said, helping the octogenarian back into her seat. When she returned to her styling station, Reesa opened the narrow drawer and pulled out a set of stapled papers. She held them up to Nyree. "Do you mean to tell me I can finally rip up this lease?"

"She told you to rip it up weeks ago," Cheyenne said. "You should know better than to doubt our girl over here. When she says she's gonna get something done, you bet your ass it's gonna get done."

Nyree hunched her shoulders in a humble shrug. "What can I say? The girl speaks the truth."

"I know I shouldn't doubt you, but I want to make sure," Reesa said. "My landlord is willing to go down to a six-month lease, but he stressed that I have until the close of business on Friday to decide. If I don't renew, I have to be out of here by mid-April."

"Any Way You Want It will be opened by the beginning of April," Nyree assured her. "Trust me."

"I do," Reesa said with an emphatic nod. "But it's easy for you to say that when you have a well-paying job at the chemical plant and steady paychecks coming in. Just remember that I live from customer-to-customer. If I don't have anywhere to do hair, I don't eat."

"You know I keep a cornbread casserole in my freezer at all times," Cheyenne said. "If you ever need it, just say the word. I'll thaw it out for you."

Reesa rolled her eyes as she picked up the needle she'd been using to sew in Cheyenne's weave. "I'm serious. It freaks me out to even think about the new place not being ready on time. That's the start of my busy season. Between prom and weddings, I work nonstop from April to the end of July. I can't afford to lose even a day."

"Yeah, and driving all the way to Metairie to work at that chiropractor clinic everyday is draining my bank account," Cheyenne said. "My local clients don't like it, either."

Just after the national chain massage company Cheyenne worked for went out of business, her friend began doing private work. A few months ago, she was nearly assaulted by a client in his home. After the incident, they'd all agreed that Cheyenne would not do any more private massages. It had been the catalyst for Nyree to stop just talking about the future and finally look into purchasing a building where they could house Any Way You Want It.

"The house is going to be ready," Nyree said. "Trust me. It's handled."

"Whatever you say, Olivia Pope."

Her girlfriends all teased her about being a mini version of the fictional crisis handler, even though—as Nyree was quick to point out—she had been handling things well before Kerry Washington's character rolled onto the scene.

"Did you go over the changes the house will need with Desmond and Lance? They aren't going to try to do all the work themselves, are they?" Reesa asked.

Nyree pulled her bottom lip between her teeth, trying to come up with the best way to tell her friends that her two older brothers, aka The Biggest Idiots East of the Mississippi, were no longer doing the renovations on the house.

Even though Desmond's unwillingness to move his schedule around for her had a lot to do with it, it wasn't the only reason her brothers were no longer overhauling Whitmer House. Nyree no longer wanted Desmond involved in the renovations because her eldest brother was a bully, plain and simple. He'd dismissed the plans Nyree and Reesa had come up with for the salon; drawing up his own vision of how they should arrange the new shampooing stations and pedicure chairs instead.

Once Nyree shot down his ideas, he'd become even more obstinate. It was typical of Desmond. If he didn't get his way, he grabbed his toys and ran home, just like a damn baby. She didn't even bother to talk to Lance about it because, when it came to their construction business, he always deferred to their older brother.

Well, those two meatheads weren't the only men in town who could hammer a nail into a wall.

Nyree had spent much of the morning calling around, looking for a new contractor. The biggest problem, of course, was finding someone within her budget who was willing to take on a job with such a tight deadline.

Yeah, she knew she was asking for a lot, but she was willing to put in the work, too. She'd made an arrangement with the supervisor of the chemical lab where she worked. She would finally use some of that paid vacation time she'd been storing up for a rainy day so that she could oversee the renovations on the house and pitch in however she could. Whatever it took to get this done in time to open by her Aunt Hazel's birthday, Nyree was willing to do it.

"No," she said, "My brothers aren't planning to do all the work on the house."

Or any *of the work on the house.*

"Good." Reesa nodded. "Because there's no way only two people will get all that work done in time for us to open in two months."

"Oh, oh, oh!" Cheyenne clapped her hands. "I just got a text from Amara."

"Is she still on location with whatever movie she's working on?" Nyree asked.

Cheyenne nodded. "She's on a quick break. She said this warmer than usual weather is giving the makeup department on the movie set fits."

"Ask her if we got the job," Reesa said.

"I am." Cheyenne's thumbs swept across the touchscreen.

Only the hum of the hairdryer could be heard as they waited for Amara's next text.

"Yes!" Cheyenne said. "Amara just heard back from the bride-to-be that she's been in contact with. She wants us to do their hair, makeup and pre-wedding massages."

"For the entire wedding party?" Reesa asked.

Cheyenne nodded. "What should I tell her?"

"The wedding is on April 9th, right?" Nyree asked. "We can handle that. Tell her to accept the job."

They all squealed again, but managed to keep their voices down this time.

Cheyenne slipped her phone back into her pocket. "I have to hand it to you, Nyree. Coming up with that package deal for weddings and bridal showers was the best idea ever."

18

Nyree made a show of patting herself on the back. Cheyenne threw a hair clip her way.

"Hey!" Nyree dodged the clip. "Can't a girl bask in her stellar idea for a moment?"

"No." Cheyenne stuck her tongue out at her.

"Either keep still or have lopsided hair. Your pick," Reesa said. She looked over at Nyree. "We still haven't decided if our signature color will be sangria or mulberry. Don't you think we need to make that decision, especially now that we'll have this entire wedding party a week after we open?"

Nyree was more concerned about the electrical system being able to handle industrial hair dryers. She'd leave deciding which shade of purple they should choose as their signature color to the other girls.

"I'll go with the majority," Nyree said.

"I just want to make sure it all looks perfect," Cheyenne said. "I've got a lot riding on this."

"We all do," Nyree reminded her. She scooted off the chair, walked over to the products she'd brought in earlier and picked up a stout bottle with a pump cap. She tossed it over to Cheyenne.

"Use this on your edges and scalp once a week. It's a combination of almond oil and rosemary. It'll keep your hair healthy under that weave."

"It won't turn my hair green, will it?"

"I haven't turned anyone's hair green since

high school," Nyree said. "I'll see y'all later. I'm meeting the real estate agent at Whitmer House. We need a special variance since we're opening a business in a residential neighborhood, so she took care of that for me. And then I need to get at least a few hours sleep before I head in to work."

"How much longer are you on nights?" Cheyenne asked.

"I still have another week. I'm good with it," Nyree said, grabbing another sucker from Reesa's workstation. "I like the nightshift. Means I have to deal with less people walking around the lab."

"I'll remember your aversion to people when you try to take over PR for the new biz," Cheyenne said.

Nyree put both hands up. "Hey, I don't necessarily like people, but people *love* me. It's my sunny personality. Wins them over every time."

Reesa and Cheyenne both hit her with the eye roll.

Nyree laughed as she draped the rain slicker on and closed the door behind her. But as she made her way back to her SUV, she couldn't stem the wave of anxiety that began to course through her.

She hadn't outright lied, but not coming clean about Desmond and Lance no longer doing the work on the house left her feeling as if she had a mixture of nitrous oxide and carbon disulfide in the pit of her stomach. There was so much riding on this new venture. Reesa, Cheyenne and Amara had entrusted her with the fate of their businesses. If she didn't come through for them, not only were their livelihoods at stake, but so were their lifelong friendships. Friendships that meant everything to her.

"You have to make this happen," Nyree whispered to herself. There was too much to lose if she didn't.

Dale Chauvin entered through the front door of Chauvin Realty and made a beeline directly for the small break room just to the right of the reception area. He waved to Lily, the new receptionist who'd started at his sister's busy real estate office a couple of months ago. As usual, she was on the phone.

Dale grabbed a can of soda from the mini fridge. Everyone in the office drank diet, but there were always a couple of cans of sugar-laden caffeine waiting for him. Just one of the ways his big sister, Vanessa, showed her love.

As he headed down the hallway of the suite of offices Vanessa shared with the other two real estate agents in her small but growing realty firm, Dale couldn't help but marvel at how much things had changed in such a short period of time. For years Vanessa had been the only real estate agent in town, but with the addition of a new outlet mall and a number of national chain retailers and restaurants, Maplesville's population had soared over the past five years. A few months ago, Vanessa realized she could no longer handle all the business suddenly heading her way on her own.

Yet, despite how busy her clients kept her, she still made time to have lunch with her little brother. They both met at their parents' home for Sunday dinner every week, but the monthly lunch was a tradition Vanessa had started back when Dale was in college. For the entire four years he attended LSU, she'd drive the hour and a half to Baton Rouge to treat him to lunch every single month, without fail.

Dale rapped on the slightly ajar door and pushed it open, finding his sister reclined in her office chair, a Bluetooth device clipped to her ear. She held up a finger to him as she listened to whoever was speaking on the other end of the line.

Dale leaned back against the wall, planting one steel-toe booted foot on the pale blue wainscoting.

"Yes, I agree. The installation of the sinks should be at the top of the list, along with the partitions for the massage area." Vanessa paused and listened. "Anyone with a background in construction can do the work you need. I'll bring you a list of contractors that my clients have worked with in the past. I'm sure one of them can meet your April deadline."

Vanessa glanced over at him. "Actually, I have someone in mind who is perfect for the job," she said. "I'll meet you at the property in fifteen minutes with the paperwork from the zoning commission. Congratulations again, Ms. Grant."

The moment she ended the call, Vanessa turned her full attention to him. "You ready for lunch?"

"As long as you remember that I'm buying this time," Dale reminded her. The fight over who would pick up the meal tab was a constant between him and his sister. She usually won, but not today.

Dale gestured to her cellphone. "So, who needs construction work done?"

"A client. I just sold her the old Whitmer House," Vanessa said.

"That big white house on Silver Oak Drive?"

Vanessa nodded. "I need to swing over there on our way to lunch to drop off this paperwork." She tapped the sheaf of papers on the desk to straighten them, then slid them into a tan envelope. "The buyer is turning the house into some sort of salon and spa. She needs a contractor to do some renovations. Of course, my first suggestion was Harding Construction, but she said they turned down the job."

"I'm not surprised," Dale said. "Harding has been moving away from those smaller jobs. There's a lot more money in the larger, industrial construction sites." He rubbed his jaw with the backs of his fingers. "I'd recommend this outfit over in St. Pierre, but the owners are a couple of assholes. I wouldn't want them to reflect badly on you if they do something to piss your client off."

"Well, I was thinking maybe *you* could do the work?" Vanessa said.

Dale stopped in the middle of drinking his Pepsi. He blew out an exhausted sigh. "We've been through this already. I'm not licensed to work on my own."

"Didn't you just renovate that Robertson man's bathroom?" she asked. She pushed away from her desk and grabbed her purse, pulling it over her shoulder.

"I changed out a sink and patched up a doorknob-size hole in the wall for Lowell Robertson."

"And look what came of it. Not only are you tutoring his kid in football, but didn't you tell me that he's interested in investing in your general contracting business — if you ever get it off the ground, that is. Seriously, Dale, why are you dragging your feet on this?"

"I'm not." God, he was tired of this conversation. "There's twenty-four hours in a day." Dale ticked items off on his fingers. "I have a fulltime job, I have the training sessions with Kendrick, Ian and I are dealing with Sam and his dad, and I do try to get at least a few hours of sleep. When am I supposed to start up a general contractor business all on my own?"

His sister folded her arms over her chest. "You could have come up with a business plan in these last few minutes you've spent explaining all the reasons why you *can't* do it. And I thought you said you wanted to cut back on some of your hours with Harding?"

Vanessa's eyes narrowed as she took a couple of steps toward him. Dale towered over her, but he could feel himself shrinking under her knowing stare.

"What are you so afraid of?" she asked.

He jerked back as if she'd plucked him in the middle of his forehead—something she used to do when he was a kid.

"What kind of question is that?"

"A legitimate one. You've been working construction for Webster Harding for nearly five years, when you should be doing it for yourself. Put that business degree to work."

Dale instantly felt his shoulders tense at the mention of his degree. A muscle twitched in his cheek.

"You said it yourself," Vanessa continued. "Harding isn't taking on smaller jobs anymore. Someone needs to fill that gap. This is the perfect time for you to branch out on your own, Dale."

When he continued to stare at her without saying anything, Vanessa threw her hands up in frustration.

"You can at least take a look at what needs to be done on the house. Who knows, maybe I'm giving you too much credit. The job probably *is* more than you can handle."

Dale huffed out a laugh. "That reverse psychology stuff stopped working on me years ago."

"Really? Crap," Vanessa said, her mouth scrunching up in a chagrinned smile.

"Come on," Dale said, "If we have to stop at the Whitmer House before lunch we need to get going. I have a training session with Kendrick after school lets out."

"We'll eat some place around here instead of going to Emile's over in Gauthier," she said.

"I'm paying," Dale reminded her.

"No, you're not."

"Yes, I am."

She pointed her finger up at him. "Stop being a little shit."

"Stop being a big bully," Dale returned.

He was tempted to bring out his favorite *you're not the boss of me* line. He hadn't used that one on her in a while. Being ten years older, Vanessa had always been the boss of him, even though she was a solid foot shorter. She'd also been his biggest champion and the kind of big sister who spoiled her little brother rotten.

And she had way more confidence in him than one person should.

"And you *are* going to take this job," she said. "My client needs a contractor and you need to use this as a way to show Lowell Robertson that he's making a good investment."

Dale dropped his shoulders and pitched his head back, releasing a dramatic sigh. When he looked at her again, he saw the determination in his sister's eyes, and he knew he'd lost this round.

He tossed his soda can in the blue recycle bin next to the door. "Can I at least drive?" he asked.

"No," Vanessa tossed over her shoulder as they left the office.

The Whitmer House was located in the older part of Maplesville—the downtown area that was currently in the midst of a resurgence now that long-time residents were no longer impressed with the strip malls, outlets and high-rise condominiums that had taken over on the outskirts of town.

Dale liked that the downtown area was getting more attention these days, but in his opinion city leaders had gone too far with the *Welcome to Mayberry* vibe. New ordinances prevented residents and businesses from adding anything that community leaders felt took away from the historic, small-town appeal. It had made for a pain in the ass when it came to finding authentic woodwork for the law office he and a couple of his buddies had renovated as a side job over on Birch Street a few months ago.

"So, any news on the girlfriend front?" Vanessa asked.

Dale frowned at her. "Why are you all up in my business today?"

"Because that's my job. Now answer the question."

He snorted. "As if I would tell you." Dale turned the Volvo's radio station from Lite Rock to NPR. Vanessa changed it right back.

"What about the girl you were seeing back at Christmas? The one with the pretty teeth. What was her name? Kathy? Casey?"

"Her name was Courtney, and I wasn't 'seeing' her," Dale said. He lowered the volume on a Billy Joel song. "We went on one date."

"You brought her to the big tree lighting ceremony. In Mama's book that means you're practically engaged. I'm sure she's already told the entire Ladies Auxiliary that a wedding is just around the corner."

"God." Dale dropped his head back on the headrest.

A couple of minutes later, Vanessa pulled up to the curb of Silver Oak Drive, in front of the stately two-story home that had belonged to the Whitmer Family for generations. This current generation obviously didn't share the nostalgia of their forefathers. None of them cared enough about the old house to keep it in the family.

Dale had always liked this house, but he hadn't given it more than a quick glance while driving by over the past couple of years. The structure's exterior was still in pretty good shape, but there were patches of green and black mold that could use a blast with the pressure-washer.

"Oh, good, she made it here already," Vanessa said.

Dale spotted a black crossover SUV parked in the driveway, close to the side entrance. That's also when he spotted the woman standing next to one of the columns on the colonnade that wrapped around the house. She had a headful of springy curls and wore blue hospital scrubs.

How had he missed *her* standing there?

Well, the fact that she couldn't be more than five-feet could explain why he hadn't noticed her at first glance, but what she lacked in height, she made up for in curves that were just subtle enough to make things interesting.

She started down the walkway, still wet from the earlier rain shower that had passed through town.

By way of greeting, Vanessa handed her the tan envelope that she'd brought from her office. "You can now legally run a salon out of this property."

"Thank you so much." She held the envelope to her chest like a kid clutching the toy she's been begging for all year long.

She was pretty cute. Okay, she was *a lot* cute.

And those curves weren't as subtle as Dale first thought. Despite her boxy clothing, he could make out a classic hourglass figure, with a chest in perfect proportion to her hips. Even so, she couldn't weigh more than a buck ten soaking wet.

At six-three and a bowl of pasta shy of two-hundred fifty pounds, Dale didn't usually gravitate toward delicate, petite women. They seemed too breakable. But delicate looked pretty nice on this one.

She turned her attention from Vanessa and set the most vibrant amber eyes on him.

"Hello," she said.

"Oh, sorry. This is my brother, Dale Chauvin," Vanessa said before he could speak. "Dale, this is Nyree Grant, the new owner of this lovely home. Dale works construction," Vanessa quickly added.

"Really?" Nyree's amber eyes widened to *Bambi* proportions.

Holy shit! He wasn't ready for the impact those eyes would have on him. She really was cute as hell.

"Yes, I do," Dale answered. "But—"

"He does *excellent* work," Vanessa continued. "Maybe we can do a quick walk-through and you can show Dale what needs to be done to the house?"

Dale cast a frustrated glare at Vanessa. She ignored it. Typical. That persistence and tenacity were what made his sister so good at her job, but he hated when she used it on him.

Vanessa started toward the house, but her client didn't follow. Nyree remained standing on the walkway. She crossed her arms, essentially creating a shelf for her breasts. Her very nice breasts. Dale couldn't help but stare. Her hospital scrubs had a V-shaped neckline. With her short frame, it revealed the most intriguing shadow between her cleavage.

He looked up to find one well-shaped brow pointed upwards.

"Are you done looking?" she asked.

"Not really," he answered without thinking. "I mean…" Dale's voice faded away when she turned and started for the front door.

Okay. It's a good thing he wasn't really trying to win this construction job, because if he had been he'd just knocked himself out of contention. Ogling your potential boss's breasts was at the top of the *Don't Do This* list.

He tried not to look at her ass as he followed her, but it drew in his gaze as if she had magnets in her back pockets. The hospital scrubs' lightweight material pulled deliciously taut across her backside. It could not be any more perfect.

When they met up with Vanessa at the home's double-door entrance, his sister's brow dipped ominously as she stared at him with a disapproving frown.

"Cut it out," she mouthed.

Dale raised his hands in a *I didn't do anything* pose, which was mostly true. Sure, her client caught him staring at her chest, but in the grand scheme of things…

Dale trailed a couple of feet behind women as they walked through the house, talking about the various tasks that would need to be done before the place was operational.

From the sound of it, this business Nyree planned to open was way more than just your normal salon. The setup she described included a retail area downstairs, as well as a place upstairs to perform holistic massage therapy — whatever the hell that was.

"And you're still planning to move in, right?" Vanessa asked.

Nyree nodded. "I have a few months remaining on my apartment lease, which should give me time to gradually move my things in upstairs."

"You're planning to live here and run a business out of this place?" Dale asked, speaking for the first time since they entered the house.

"Actually, there will be several businesses," she said. "Me and my three best friends from high school are combining our businesses into a one-stop salon and spa." She ticked them off on her fingers. "Hair, massage, makeup and a storefront for my line of hair and skincare products. And, yeah, I plan to live here too."

Vanessa spoke. "The layout of the house is actually perfect for it. There's a hallway separating the upstairs parlor and two bedrooms, and a service stairway that leads directly to the kitchen. The house can be filled with customers and Nyree would never have to worry about running into any of them."

"Of course, there's a lot that needs to happen before we can get any customers in here," Nyree said. "And finding a contractor to do the work has been the biggest pain in the ass ever."

Vanessa turned to him. "Which is why I brought—" she started, but then her phone rang. She glanced at the smart watch on her wrist. "Excuse me, but I need to take this," she said before stepping into the hallway.

Dale stood in the center of the room with his hands on his hips and a dozen thoughts muddling around in his brain. He shouldn't care one way or the other what type of renovations needed to be done to this place. He wasn't licensed to do the work.

"You said you want to put in three sinks for shampooing down here, along with a couple of those chairs they have in nail salons, right?" Dale asked, despite the fact that he definitely was *not* doing the work on this house.

"Pedicure chairs," Nyree answered with a nod. "But those will be in Amara's space over on the left side of the house—she's the makeup artist," she explained. "She doesn't do the actual manicures and pedicures; she has a girl who works with her. Not that you care about any of that," she said with a nervous laugh.

That revealing chuckle hit him square in the chest. Dale had thought she was cute from the moment he first saw her, but knowing he made her nervous upped the cuteness factor to ridiculous levels.

It was even more of a reason to back away from this job. Not only was he not licensed to take on a construction project of this scale, but if he wanted to explore all the other possible ways he could make Nyree smile he sure as hell couldn't work for her.

But damn if his mind wasn't fixated on figuring out how he could make this space work as a salon. Vanessa knew exactly what she was doing when she brought him here.

Dale walked over to the room on the opposite end of the vestibule that took up the center of the home's first level. He went back and forth between the two spaces several times, mentally arranging the layout.

Nyree slinked in next to him. "So, what are you thinking?"

"This room is adjacent to the downstairs bathroom," Dale said, pointing to the larger room that Nyree said would house the hair salon. "If you install the sinks on this side, you can easily tie them into the existing plumbing."

"That's exactly what my brother suggested." She pulled her bottom lip between her teeth and Dale lost his train of thought. With that move, she'd surged right past cute and tumbled headfirst into the sexy-as-hell category.

"I get what you're saying," she said, knocking him out of his temporary daze. "The only problem is that we really wanted the shampooing stations on this side so that the styling chairs could be here, facing the windows. It would provide the customers with such a beautiful view of the azaleas on the side lawn."

"What's more important to you? A pretty

view for your customers or installing several thousand dollars of extra plumbing work that'll tack on at least another two weeks to the length of the job?"

She tipped her head to the side, thinking. A wry grin slowly formed across her lips. "I'll find a nice picture to hang on the wall," Nyree said.

He laughed. "Thought so."

She folded her arms across her chest and studied him for a moment. "So, you work construction full-time?"

Dale nodded.

"Are you any good?"

A smile edged up one side of Dale's mouth. "I'm very good," he answered.

Her gaze dropped to his chest before she focused on his face again. One well-trimmed eyebrow arched as amusement glittered in her amber eyes.

"Am I supposed to just take your word for it?"

"You want a demonstration?"

She shrugged. "It would be nice if you could show me what you can do before I hire you."

"Who says I'm available?"

She pulled that supple bottom lip between her teeth again as her eyes swept the length of his body. "What would it take to make you available?"

He stepped up to her. "Depends."

"On?"

"On what you're willing to do for my

services."

That brow cocked again. "If you're as good as you say you are, then I'm willing to do just about anything for it, whatever the cost. As far as I'm concerned, everything's negotiable."

Dale surreptitiously sucked in a breath. This no longer felt like lighthearted flirting. This seemed more like 'let's go to a movie, grab dinner and then back to my place' territory. He could work with that.

"Sorry about the call," Vanessa said, coming in from the hallway. Her return had the same effect as a blast of freezing cold air hitting his face. Nothing worked better at putting the kibosh on his tempted libido than having his big sister around.

Dale backed up several feet and stuck his hands in his front pockets. "I...um...I can show you that place a couple of blocks down on Birch if you want to see samples of my work," he said.

"Does that mean you'll do the renovations?" Nyree asked.

Wait? Had he said that?

"Of course he'll do the renovations," Vanessa said.

Shit. "Wait." Dale held both hands up.

"Please," Nyree said. It was the desperation in her plea that did him in. "I'm running out of time," she said. "I'm willing to pay five percent over the going rate if it means you can start as soon as possible."

"Can I at least have a day to get you an

estimate?" Dale asked.

What was he saying? He couldn't take on this job.

"Yes." Nyree nodded emphatically. She hooked a thumb toward the door. "I have an extra copy of the design plan and renovation blueprints in my car. You can take them with you to figure out the estimate."

Tell her no.

"Okay," Dale said instead.

The smart thing would be to take a day or two to think this over. This job would require more time away from his job at Harding Construction than the smaller side jobs he'd worked on in the past. He should take a step back, tell Nyree that he needed to think about this first.

But he didn't. And he wouldn't. Because the thought of dimming the cautious hope shining in her amber eyes made Dale's stomach hurt.

"You want to meet back here the same time tomorrow?" Dale asked.

Her entire face lit up with her smile, and Dale knew he was toast.

"Keep in mind that I'm not officially licensed with the Louisiana Licensing Board for Contractors," he cautioned.

"But you've done this type of work before, right?"

"Yes, he has," Vanessa said. "He's worked construction with Maplesville's biggest contractor for the past five years. He can handle this job. And he'll be licensed with the state soon enough."

"As long as we're up and running by April 4th, I don't care when you get your license." Nyree turned to Vanessa. "Thank you so much. I was at the end of my rope."

"You're welcome," his sister returned, her face beaming like a fairy godmother who'd just made someone's wishes come true. "Congratulations again. I wish you the best with your new business."

"Once we're officially open you'll have a day of pampering on the house." Nyree glanced at her watch. "I need to get some sleep before I go in to work tonight. Let me get those blueprints for you." She motioned for them to follow her out of the house. Once at her SUV, she grabbed a cardboard mailing tube from the backseat and handed it to Dale.

"One of the biggest tasks will be partitioning two of the upstairs bedrooms into four individual massage areas." She said as she followed him and Vanessa to where they'd parked on the curb. "You'll see it when you look at the blueprints."

His sister climbed into the driver's side, but Dale remained standing. He reached into his back pocket and pulled out his phone. He handed it to Nyree.

"You mind putting your number in there?" he asked.

That subtle, sexy smile curved up the corner

of her lips again. "It's usually a lot harder for a guy to get my number," she said, her thumbs gliding swiftly across the touchscreen. She handed the phone back to him. "My shift ends at seven a.m., so if you have the estimate ready ahead of time, just text me. I can be here by eight tomorrow morning."

"I'll bring coffee," Dale said, his own smile forming.

"Two sugars, one cream. See you tomorrow," she said before turning on her heel and heading back for the house.

Dale watched her as she walked away. When he got in the car, his sister immediately slapped him upside the head.

"Hey," he said, rubbing the side of his head. "What's that about?"

"Just knocking some sense into that head of yours, since you obviously lost what little you had. She's technically your boss now."

"I haven't agreed to take the job just yet."

"But you *will* take the job," Vanessa said in a voice that brooked no argument. Bossy as hell, per usual. "That means," she continued as she started the car. "No more of that staring at her ass thing you've been doing since we got here."

Dale strapped the seatbelt over his chest and looked over at his sister. "Are you jealous because you want her for yourself?" he asked.

She snorted. "As if I would ever be unprofessional enough to date a client," Vanessa said. "Which is something *you* have to consider now that you're taking this job."

"Hey, I'm not an official contractor, right? So all that professional decorum shit shouldn't apply to me."

She drilled him with a death stare. "I recommended you, so whatever you do will reflect on me. Keep it professional," she said as she pulled away from the curb.

Chapter Two

"No, no, no. You need to hold your core steady," Dale instructed. He patted his own abs. "Right here. Make sure this is nice and tight. Think of it as your anchor." He walked around to Kendrick Robertson's back and clamped his hands on the six-foot-tall teenager's shoulders. "Keep your shoulders forward, your hips tilted just so, and your legs steady."

Dale walked back around the high school junior and faced him. He stared at the boy as he assumed the pose Dale had perfected over the years as a middle linebacker. He'd started honing it when he was still in elementary school and playing in the Pop Warner league with his two best friends, Ian Landry and Sam Stewart.

"I'm going to count to three," Dale said. "On three, you charge." Dale held up his stopwatch. "One, two, three."

Kendrick moved with a swiftness he hadn't possessed a month ago when Dale first started working with him. The kid had taken everything he'd taught him so far and used it to improve his reaction time, agility and speed.

The circumstances that led to Dale accepting this training gig still had him scratching his head. A buddy of his from Harding Construction had taken on a side job for Lowell Robertson, but came down with a bad flu that put him out of commission. He'd asked Dale to step in for him.

When Dale showed up for the job the following morning, he'd been taken aback by Lowell Robertson's excitement. The man's effusive gushing had been so over-the-top that, for a moment, Dale had honestly thought he'd walked into an elaborate prank set up by Ian and Sam. But it wasn't a joke. Robertson was just a huge football fan, and revered Dale as one of the best middle linebackers to come out of this area in the last twenty years.

While Dale installed his new toilet, Robertson had regaled him with a running commentary on the local high school football scene, which his son, Kendrick, was a part of. He'd ranted about the boy's varsity team losing out in the first round of the high school playoffs this past season. That's when Robertson had come up with the idea to have Dale tutor Kendrick.

Dale initially turned him down. He'd stepped away from football after the injury that had changed the course of his life back in his senior year of college. Other than watching the occasional game on Sunday afternoons, Dale had tried his best to stay away from the action.

Besides, he could tell from the outset that Lowell Robertson fit the mold of Obnoxious

Football Dad, the kind who attended every practice and loved putting his two cents in where it didn't belong. Dale would bet the man had Kendrick's high school coach popping antacids on a daily basis.

But Robertson was persistent. Dale eventually caved, but with the stipulation that these one-on-one training sessions be exactly that. He didn't want Lowell standing over his shoulder, critiquing everything he did. He thought it would be a deal breaker, but Robertson was willing to put up with Dale's conditions if it meant his son could work with the best.

He'd kept this training gig under wraps. He hadn't even told his father, only Sam, Ian and Vanessa. He didn't want it getting out that he was training someone who played for the Wildcats of Magnolia Bend High, another of the Maplesville Mustangs' rivals. If the people here knew Dale was tutoring one of the enemies, he'd never live it down. If there was one thing folks in this town took seriously, it was their high school football.

"That's good," Dale said, satisfied with the kid's stance. He motioned Kendrick to follow him over to where he'd set up short orange cones in the shape of a big letter T. "Time for some T-drills," Dale said.

Kendrick responded with a quick nod and immediately began the classic drill used to test agility. He sprinted and shuffled from one cone to the other, tapping the top before going to the next.

Dale had to admit the kid was good. He was also disciplined and didn't complain, no matter how hard Dale pushed him. When he looked at Kendrick, he saw someone who didn't just play for the hell of it. He played because he loved the sport and recognized that it was a privilege to play the game at this level.

It was scary how much of himself he saw in this kid.

It had been so long since he'd had anything to do with football other than watching it as a spectator. These few training sessions with Kendrick had reignited the spark. He hadn't realized just how much he missed it.

He needed this game in his life.

Over the past month he'd spent more time studying mock plays to act out with Kendrick than the blueprints of the construction jobs he'd been working on at Harding. But Dale knew this football training thing was temporary. When he wasn't here with Kendrick, his focus should be on the job that paid the bills.

And with the offer he'd gotten from Lowell Robertson a couple of weeks ago, the idea of starting his own small general contractor business was looking more and more like it could become reality. Dale still wasn't sure if the man had offered to become an investor because he actually believed he did quality work, or because he was still star struck. It shouldn't matter one way or the other to him. As long as Robertson was willing to put up the money, that's all Dale needed to be concerned with.

If he could start up his own business, Dale had no doubt it would thrive. Nyree's difficulty in finding a contractor to renovate the Whitmer House illustrated the need for a smaller outfit in Maplesville. Working construction may not be as glamorous as the NFL career he'd always dreamed of, but it had remained steady despite the dips in the housing market, and he was good at it.

Dale swallowed down the bitter tang that instantly filled his mouth.

If someone had told him ten years ago that becoming a general contractor would be the highlight of his life, Dale would have laughed in their faces and told them to piss off. But that's where things stood right now. This wasn't what he'd imagined for himself, but he only had himself to blame for the way things had turned out. He was living with the consequences of the choices he'd made years ago. Choices he regretted more than anything in the world.

Nyree pulled in behind an old pickup truck that sat in the driveway at Whitmer House. She made out the shape of Dale's head on the driver's side moments before the door opened and he alighted from the truck. As he walked toward her car carrying two paper coffee cups, Nyree concentrated on taking a couple of deep breaths. Apparently the insta-lust she experienced after meeting him yesterday wasn't just a one-time thing.

It was the way he carried himself. That understated confidence wrapped in a strikingly gorgeous package of toned muscles, light brown skin, and a devastating smile. It was hard not to be a bit overwhelmed.

She climbed from behind the wheel of her SUV and met him at her front bumper.

"Sorry I'm late," Nyree said by way of greeting. "I had some paperwork to finish up at the end of my shift and lost track of time."

"I only got here five minutes ago myself," he said, handing her a paper cup. "Two sugars, one cream."

"You remembered." She couldn't have contained the smile that blossomed across her lips if her life had depended on it. "Thank you. I'm sure I'll need at least three more of these to make it through the rest of the morning."

"Rough shift at the hospital?"

Nyree's forehead creased in a frown. "Huh?"

He reached over and fingered the hem of her sleeve. "I assumed you worked at Maplesville General."

"Oh, the scrubs," she said. She took a sip of coffee, needing the brief pause to bring her heart rate back under control after his light touch.

"They're not just for people in the medical field, you know?" she continued with a laugh. "I'm a chemist at Lakeshore Oil Refinery. We wear scrubs in the lab because we deal with chemicals that will ruin a nice shirt in three seconds flat."

She paused to release an embarrassingly long yawn.

"Oh, wow. Excuse me," Nyree said.

Dale's eyes narrowed. "Are you sure you don't want to take a nap? I can come back later."

She shook her head. "No. The sooner you can get started, the better. Do you have the estimate?"

He pulled a set of folded papers from his back pocket, but he didn't hand it over. Instead, he tapped it against his thigh, the paper rasping against the fabric of his faded blue jeans.

"Before we go over this I want to make sure I included all the renovations you have in mind. Are you okay with doing another walk-through before we discuss price?" Dale asked.

"Of course," she said, motioning for him to follow her.

As they made their way through each room, Nyree gave him a more detailed explanation of everything she envisioned.

"I want the experience to be seamless for the people who choose to do an entire day of pampering. That means they move from their massage with Cheyenne, to a facial and makeup application with Amara, and finally into one of the chairs in Reesa's hair salon without missing a beat."

He nodded while making notes on a spiral bound notepad he'd pulled from his pocket. They made their way upstairs, into the rooms that would become Cheyenne's massage center.

Dale stood in the middle of one of the empty bedrooms that faced the front of the house. "According to the blueprints, you want to divide these two front bedrooms into four individual massage areas and a small lobby, but you don't indicate the level of soundproofing you want in the two additional walls I'll have to erect. I've never had a massage in a spa before, but I assume peace and quiet is a part of the experience."

"It's a huge part," Nyree said. She hadn't considered soundproofing, and, of course, Cheyenne hadn't mentioned it. Her friends were more concerned about aesthetics; they weren't thinking about wall insulation. "What are my options?" she asked.

He hunched his shoulders in a casual shrug. "There's a pretty broad range—from basic padding that should at least muffle voices, to top of the line soundproofing material that'll let you scream at the top of your lungs without the person in the next room hearing a sound."

She laughed. "There shouldn't be any screaming going on. It's not that kind of massage parlor." She tipped her head to the side. "Although we'd make a lot more money if it were."

One corner of his mouth curved up in amusement. "No doubt," he said. "But probably not worth the weekly police raids."

"Probably not," she answered with a grin.

Several beats passed as they stood there staring at each other. Nyree nervously pulled her bottom lip between her teeth. She noticed the way Dale's eyes tracked the movement. He studied her mouth, his breaths becoming more labored.

With a sudden shake of his head, he cleared his throat and took a step back. "So, the soundproofing," he said.

"Yes, the soundproofing." She nodded. It took her a moment to remember what they were talking about. "Uh, what do you recommend?"

"It all depends on what you're willing to spend on the materials."

"Actually, it depends on whatever will take the least amount of time." Nyree held her hands up. "Don't get me wrong, I have to take price into consideration, but making sure everything is ready by our April 4th grand opening means more to me than saving a couple of dollars." She looked up at him. "I know it's going to take a miracle to get the amount of work that needs to be done completed in just two months. Are you sure this is something you can handle?"

"What if I say that I can't?" he asked. "What are your options then?"

Nyree's stomach dropped, because she knew she didn't have many options. She'd searched online last night for contractors, hoping to find someone she'd missed in her initial search, just in case Dale fell through. There was no one else. She'd exhausted the list of contractors in this area.

But 'can't' had never been a part of her vocabulary, and Nyree wouldn't allow it to sneak in there now.

"I'll find a way to get it done," she said. "I have to. It's just that simple."

His brow cocked with a look of amused admiration. "You're pretty determined."

"I don't fail," Nyree said. "Especially when it comes to something so important."

Dale backed up to the wall and leaned on it, crossing his arms over his broad chest.

"Here's what I don't understand," he said. "According to Vanessa, you convinced the Whitmer family to go through an accelerated closing on the house. What if they hadn't agreed to that? What would you have done then about this grand opening that's supposed to happen in two months?"

"I never considered not being able to close on the house," she said without a shred of compunction. "I needed it to happen, so I made sure it did. Like you said, I'm pretty determined."

"I guess so," he replied, that smile stretching wider. "So why are you so tied to this date? What's so special about April 4th?"

Nyree knew the question was coming, yet it

still pained her to answer. She pulled in a deep breath. "It was my Aunt Hazel's birthday," she said. "She died two years ago. Breast cancer."

"I'm sorry."

"Thank you," Nyree said. She was proud of the way she held her composure. Even after two years, the ache from losing her aunt was still raw.

"She was a special woman," Nyree continued. "Actually, she's the inspiration behind this entire business, which is why it's really important to me that it opens on her birthday."

He nodded. "I'll make sure that happens."

"Are you sure? I can continue to look for someone who can help."

He shook his head. "I have my own set of men that I work with. If there's work to be done that I can't handle on my own, I'll subcontract one of them." He pulled out the estimate. "These numbers are based on you changing the arrangement of the three shampoo stations in the salon area. I can easily tie in the plumbing myself, but if you decide to reroute it to fit with your original plan, I'll have to hire my buddy Leon. I'd feel more comfortable with someone who's had more experience with plumbing than I have."

"It's encouraging to know that you wouldn't bite off more than you can chew for the sake of being macho."

"I am macho," he said with a grin. "But I'm

not stupid. I know my limits."

That smile. Goodness. It killed her!

"I, uh…" Nyree cleared her throat. "I talked to Reesa and she's okay with the shampoo stations being on the opposite side. Not as if she had much choice," Nyree said. "When it comes to the house, the buck stops with me. My friends are paying rent, but I'm the one who bought this place."

"Impressive," he said.

"Is it?"

"You don't think so?"

Nyree shrugged. "It's something I've always wanted to do."

"And once you decide to do something, you do it."

"You're a quick learner," she quipped.

His lips eased into a subtle, yet sexy grin, while amusement shimmered in his warm brown eyes. "So, are we making this thing official?" he asked.

"Do you want it to be?"

The humor in his gaze turned to heat as his eyes dropped to her mouth. "Yeah," Dale said. "I want it."

Warmth instantly spread throughout her body, the flush of heat so powerful Nyree was surprised small flames didn't erupt along her skin.

"Are we still talking about the job?" she asked.

Dale's head jerked up. "Uh, yeah." He took

a step back. "Wait. I'm sorry, what were you asking?"

She so wanted to call him on his previous slip, but decided against it. There was work to be done.

"How soon can you start?" she asked instead.

"I'll put in the order for the building materials as soon as we're done here, then come back in a few hours to start measuring out where the shampoo stations will go. I want to tackle that first."

"What about your other job?" she asked. "Don't you work full-time for Harding Construction?"

"The project I'm currently working on with Harding is scheduled to wrap up in the next couple of days. Once that's done, I'm all yours."

Nyree pulled her bottom lip between her teeth.

She knew he didn't mean it in the same way her mind heard it, but that didn't stop the heated tingle that skirted along her skin.

"I like the sound of that," she said. "I'll see you in a few hours."

Chapter Three

Dale glanced at his watch as he single-handily lifted the 4 x 8 foot sheet of fiberboard and carried it over to his boss. He was counting down the seconds to 3:00 p.m., when the second shift was scheduled to relieve the guys who'd come on the construction site at six o'clock this morning. This was his final day on this job, and he was more than ready to commit full-time to Nyree.

To the job. He was ready to commit to *the job* he was doing for Nyree.

Webster Harding stared in disgust at the building material Dale stacked against the wall.

"I tried to convince Lou to go with the cypress, but he's a stubborn son of a bitch," Harding said. "This fiberboard crap will rot out in a couple of years."

Dale shrugged. "It's treated. With proper care it should be okay."

"Don't say that too loud, Chauvin. I'm trying to make money here," his boss said.

Dale just shook his head as he returned to the stacks of fiberboard they were using for the interior walls of the motel being erected just outside of Maplesville proper. He knew it killed his boss that the property owner refused to bend on the materials.

Harding was a grade-A charmer with a head for turning a profit. That was the reason his construction company was the most successful in Maplesville. Harding talked a good game when it came to convincing clients that he would deliver the best in craftsmanship. Dale had had to bite his tongue more than once as he listened to Harding persuade a client into believing that his company was worth the expense. The fact of the matter was, not everyone could afford the very best of the best. A customer shouldn't feel obligated to break the bank in order to get some decent construction work done on their homes and businesses.

That's where *his* new contractor business could fit in. He wouldn't try to pressure anyone into paying for anything they couldn't afford. The people around here needed someone who was willing to work within a client's budget and still give them a quality product.

"Great," Dale whispered under his breath when he realized it was exactly what Vanessa tried to tell him. As if he needed another reason for his sister to say 'I told you so.'

It should come as no surprise that Vanessa was right, although Dale wasn't about to tell her that. She'd been extra smug this past week, gloating over him accepting the job with Nyree, as if she'd single-handedly made it happen.

Okay, so maybe she had. And he couldn't deny that Vanessa had a point about this being the perfect opportunity for him to get his own general contractor business off the ground, especially now that he had an investor interested in backing him up with much needed capital. Maplesville needed someone to fill in the gap between high-end outfits like Harding Construction and run-of-the-mill handymen who did construction work as a side job.

He could be that alternative.

Yet, even as he considered what it would feel like to hang an open sign above his own general contractor business, Dale couldn't help but acknowledge the trace of unease that skidded down his spine. He'd done everything he could to convince himself that this is what he wanted, but it was hard to believe in that lie when he had to fight back a panic attack at the thought of actually going through with it.

There was a difference between *wanting* to do something, and believing that you *have* to do it because it's the only thing you're good at. He was good at working construction. He could have been good at a lot more, if he hadn't wasted the opportunities he'd been given years ago.

Dale's hands tightened on the two-by-fours he'd just lifted from the pallet of building materials. If he had a nickel for every regret he harbored, he wouldn't have to work another day of his life.

Twenty minutes later, he climbed into his truck and pulled onto the highway, heading for downtown Maplesville. He was officially done with the motel job. He'd talked it over with Webster, and just as Dale had anticipated, his boss had no problem with him taking a couple of months off to work on Nyree's project. There were always guys clamoring to join Harding Construction. The pay was good and the work was steady.

Harding assured him that there would be a spot for him when he was done renovating the Whitmer House, but maybe he wouldn't need that spot. Maybe this really was the kick in the pants he needed to finally get his own business off the ground.

It was a testament to some of the good he'd done in his life that he'd get this chance to prove himself while working in the presence of Nyree Grant.

Dale tightened his fingers around the steering wheel, fighting the pent up lust coursing through him just at the thought of seeing her in a few minutes. These past five days had been an exercise in maintaining his control unlike any he'd ever been through before. She told him she'd be around the house while he worked, but he didn't realize how much she'd be around.

Granted, she'd spent most of her time on the other side of the house, painting the walls of the rooms that would house the makeup studio, but she didn't have to be right next to him for Dale to know she was there. He could feel her presence in the air. It was the hardest thing in the world to concentrate knowing she was just a room away, dressed in those boxy hospital scrubs that still managed to be sexy as hell.

Dale pulled up to the Whitmer House and grabbed his toolbox from the lock box in the bed of his truck. The rain that had been falling off and on for most of the day started to drizzle once again. As he approached the home's side entrance, he could hear Nyree singing in that adorable off-key voice he'd already become used to. There were a few guys at the construction site who sang or hummed while they worked, and it always irritated the hell out of him. Funny how he found it cute whenever Nyree did it.

She stood in the middle of the kitchen, her back turned to him as she painted the trim work she'd been working on for the past five days. The hardwood floors were covered with a plastic drop cloth. Two sawhorses were spaced evenly apart. Positioned across them were several long pieces of the pre-primed baseboards that would go around the flooring of the entire house.

"Rain ran you inside?" Dale asked.

She turned at the sound of his voice. "Hey," she said. "I didn't hear you come in."

"Hard to hear over that angelic voice," he teased.

"Ha   ha.   Very   funny."   Her   rather

inharmonious singing had already become a standing joke between them. She set her paintbrush on the edge of the paint tray and folded her arms across her chest.

"So, are you officially all mine?" she asked in an innocent voice, as if the words weren't dripping in innuendo. The mischievous smile playing at the edge of her lips was so damn tempting it made his skin heat.

Dale knew he would eventually have to put an end to this flirting. It had been okay—even expected—the day they first met. How could two single people who were obviously attracted to each other not flirt?

But now that he was working for her, it was unprofessional. Not only was it unprofessional, it was also dangerous as hell. Because the more they flirted, the more he wanted it to become something beyond the teasing, sometimes downright suggestive, banter they'd shared these past few days.

Yet, despite knowing that he shouldn't do it, Dale held his hands out and answered her previous question. "That's right, boss," he said. "I'm all yours."

Her eyes traveled the length of him. "Hmm, now that I have you full time, I'm going to have to really put you to work. You know that, right?"

"What have I been doing for the past five days? Playing around?" he asked as he took off his jacket and clipped his tool belt around his waist.

"Oh, you've been putting in the work, but time is running out," she said. "We're down to seven weeks."

He stepped up to her. "You don't think I can handle it?"

"You haven't shown me everything you can do just yet."

Dale pulled in a deep breath. "You know, when I took this job my sister told me I'd have to act professionally."

"Meaning?"

"Meaning no thinking about you the way I'm thinking about you right now."

Her heated eyes glittered with amusement. "So what does it say about me if I'm thinking the same about you?"

He grinned. "You're technically my boss. I think that means I can sue you for sexual harassment."

Nyree burst out laughing. "I've spent all my money on this house. If you tried to sue me, I'm afraid there's not much I have left to give."

"We could think of something," he said.

His chest heaved with the breaths he sucked in as he tried to find his center of control. They were playing a dangerous game, but one he was willing to lose if it meant succumbing to this attraction that had been raging out of control for nearly a week.

Yet whenever he thought about broaching the subject, something made him back off. No, it wasn't just *some*thing, it was one thing in particular.

He was intimidated by her.

Dale wasn't ashamed to admit it. How could he not be at least a little intimidated when faced with a woman as accomplished as Nyree. He'd never met anyone so young who had their shit together the way she did. Hell, she'd achieved more than a lot of people he knew who were twice her age. What did he have to offer someone like Nyree? Other than the obvious.

Then again, maybe that's all she wanted from him. She sure as hell didn't look interested in his brain when she stared at him like she wanted to have him for dinner.

But if there's one thing Dale wasn't up for, it was playing stud. He'd been down that road before, dating women who were more interested in the fact that he was a big, brawny football player with the body and reputation to match. He could still remember the way it made him feel, like a piece of meat that wasn't good for anything other than getting them off. He may only be a construction worker with a used pickup truck and dust on his steel-toe boots, but that didn't mean he had to go back to being arm candy for women who were out of his league.

And, let's face it, Nyree was out of his league. At least he could acknowledge it.

He hooked his thumb over his shoulder. "I should probably get to work," he said. "I want to have the rest of the piping done by the time the shampoo bowls arrive tomorrow."

Her reluctance was evident in the way her shoulders slumped, but she nodded and went back to painting the baseboards.

Dale spent the next hour fighting back the urge to slip into the kitchen just so he could see her. He'd come up with a dozen inane excuses he could use, but every single one of them was more transparent than the lace curtains that used to hang in his grandmother's sewing room.

Why was he wasting his time thinking up excuses? He should just go in there and lay everything on the table. Forget being professional. Forget not being good enough for her. Who in the hell cared whether or not he was good enough for her? If all she wanted from him was a nice piece of ass that could get her off, he could live with that.

"Hey, you got a minute?"

Dale jerked the miter saw so hard he slipped, having to stop himself with his hand on the floor.

"Shit," he cursed.

"Sorry," Nyree said as she approached. "You didn't hurt yourself, did you?"

Only his pride. "Nah, I'm good," Dale said. "You needed something?"

She nodded. "I can't believe I forgot to tell you about this," she said. "Okay, so I told you about my Aunt Hazel and how she's the inspiration for this salon and spa, right?"

"Yeah," he said.

"Well, if it's possible, I'd like to incorporate her old counter and chair into the new business, as something of a memorial to her. I was thinking it could go in the vestibule."

"I don't see why not. You're using the vestibule as the customer check-in, right? It'll save you from having to build a counter from scratch."

"My brother is convinced that the chair and counter won't fit in the space, but I think it's just that he doesn't think it will look good there. Granted, it's pretty beat up and stained, but it was my Aunt Hazel's. My girlfriends and I used to hang out in her shop everyday after school. We all would really love to have this little piece of her in the new place."

"I'd have to take a look at it to make sure."

"It's in the shed over at my grandmother's. It'll only take about twenty minutes to drive to St. Pierre."

Dale checked his watched. "Give me a few minutes to finish this up."

"I need to wash up myself," she said. "My mom just called to remind me that she made the lasagna I've been begging her to make for the past two weeks." She tipped her head to the side. "You're welcome to join us for dinner," she said.

He hated lasagna, but he'd be damned if he passed up an invitation to dinner from Nyree.

"Sure. Thanks," he said.

Dale shook his head. He knew this wasn't a

good idea, but he no longer cared.

Just as he started to pack up his tools, his phone chimed with an incoming text message. It was from Ian Landry, one of his best friends from high school. Dale wasn't surprised to see that the text was about Sam Stewart, his other best friend.

Meet me at Sam's? He needs company tonight.

Dale dropped his chin to his chest. Well, there went dinner.

"Shit," he released an exhausted sigh.

The past eight months had been hell for Sam, but it wasn't until this past holiday season that it finally hit home.

Sam's dad was dying.

The realization that this past Christmas was the last one his dad would see had hit Sam particularly hard. To be honest, it hadn't been easy for Ian and Dale, either. Charlie Stewart had been the cool dad when they were growing up. He'd been the dad who took them all fishing, who let them watch R-rated movies in the little shed he'd fixed up in their backyard before man caves were even a thing, the dad who'd given them all their first sips of beer before they were old enough to drink.

Dale had always had a great relationship with his own father, but it was different from the connection they all had with Charlie. When it came to Martin Chauvin, Dale's main goal had always been to make him proud. He wanted his dad to look at him and feel honored that he had

Dale as a son.

It wasn't like that with Charlie. He'd never felt the pressure to always be the best or feel as if he had to earn respect. Charlie Stewart just let his boys be boys, and had taken great pride in the young men they'd become.

Watching the once robust man wither away from ALS was one of the hardest things Dale had ever had to witness. Now that the end was near, both he and Ian tried to be there for Sam as much as possible.

He texted Ian back: *Give me an hour.*

That should be enough time to drive over to St. Pierre and back to Maplesville.

Dale heard footsteps coming down the spiral stairs that led from the kitchen to the upstairs rooms where Nyree planned to live once the renovation was complete. Over the past week she'd brought over a few pieces of furniture, clothes and some toiletries.

She came back into the salon dressed in a pair of weathered jeans and a long-sleeved t-shirt.

"Are you ready?" she said.

Dale's lips tipped up in a grin. "I'm all yours."

Nyree lost count of the number of times she looked back in her rearview mirror at Dale's pickup truck. Every time their eyes connected his lips would lift in that sexy half smile that had the same effect as lighting a match directly to her blood. The man was driving her insane with his ridiculous levels of hotness.

I'm all yours.

She knew it was just an expression—one that had become a running joke between them. But hearing those words from him yet again—combined with the industrial-strength flirting that had gone on between them over the past five days—had her skin itching with the need to pull over, drag him into her car, and climb aboard those muscular thighs.

This is what happened when one was in the midst of an eight-month drought.

And it wasn't as if she'd had her world rocked every night even *before* she and her last boyfriend, Calvin, broke up. Nyree could admit that she and Calvin had not been a good match from the very start. She probably would have broken things off with him long before she did, if it wasn't for her two older brothers demanding that she stop seeing him. When Desmond and Lance found out that Calvin, a mechanical engineer at the refinery, was ten years older than her, they'd both gone ballistic. She'd kept Calvin around particularly to show those two meatheads that they had no say over whom she dated.

It wasn't the smartest move, because in the end, she was the one who'd suffered. Calvin's idea of a good time was going to state parks on the weekends to bird watch. Nyree had nothing against bird watching, but every damn weekend?

And that was nothing compared to how boring he was in the bedroom. As in start-and-finish-before-the-commercials-were-over boring. She didn't know a single thing about Dale's bedroom skills, but she'd bet her brand new shipment of therapeutic peppermint oil that he'd last through more than a few commercials.

She glanced in the rearview mirror again and wondered how long she'd have to wait before she got the chance to find out for herself.

Her hands tightened on the steering wheel as she released an irritated groan. She was both confounded and frustrated by the intensity of her attraction to him. Getting involved with anyone, even in a casual relationship, should be the very last thing on her mind right now. Between work, stocking up inventory for her retail shop, and making sure Any Way You Want It was ready for their swiftly approaching grand opening, she didn't have time to even think about her love life.

Certain parts of her body disagreed. The minute Dale came around her libido lit up like the massive Christmas tree at Rockefeller Center.

Most surprising—and unnerving—was how far his appeal went beyond just the physical. Maybe if he'd left just one of the boxes on her list unchecked, the temptation wouldn't be so incredibly strong. But he didn't. So far, he'd marked off every single one.

Single. Employed. Respectful. Sense of Humor. Good-looking. And, okay, he deserved three checks for sexy.

That firm-enough-to-bounce-a-quarter-off-of-it ass wasn't even on her list, but he'd checked that box, too. His huge, broad shoulders and those remarkably solid thighs just added to his overall appeal.

But it was so much more than just his looks. She appreciated that he could hold a conversation about something beyond sports and cars. In fact, he had her rethinking her position on several political issues after the discussion they had yesterday while cutting the holes in the floor for the pipes that would be installed later this week. Dale stimulated her mind as well as her body.

But, *my goodness*, did he stimulate her body.

Nyree squeezed her thighs together.

"That vibrator's gonna get a workout tonight," she muttered under her breath.

She'd have to rely on assuaging her needs on her own, because Dale seemed content to stick with the flirting and nothing more. Even though they hadn't discussed it outright, there seemed to be an unspoken understanding between them that things remain strictly professional.

Nyree still wasn't sure how she felt about that. She knew it was probably for the best. Both she and Dale needed to focus on the renovation. But, dammit, it's not as if they worked on the house twenty-four-seven. Why couldn't there be something more between them during the downtime?

She looked back to make sure he was still behind her and flipped on the turning signal as she approached the graveled driveway of her grandmother's tiny clapboard house on Paulina Street in St. Pierre. Nyree had lived here, along with her mother and her brothers, since her parent's divorce back when she was ten years old.

If there was one thing this house never lacked, it was people. Enough places for all those people to sleep? Now that was a different story. With only two bedrooms, Desmond and Lance spent their teenage years flipping coins to see who would get to sleep on the sofa and who had to take the floor.

A couple of years ago, Nyree combined her tax refund and Christmas bonus and bought building materials so that Desmond and Lance could build another bathroom onto the house. When she finally started to turn a profit from her skin and hair care line, she would have her brothers finally remodel the kitchen.

Nyree got out of her SUV and waited for Dale to pull up behind her. She'd called her mom on the drive over to let her know that she was on her way, but would be going straight to the shed behind the house. It was a preemptive move to prevent the conniption fit both her mother and grandmother would have if she came to the house without going inside to say hello first.

She stared as Dale climbed out of his pickup truck, and that persistent case of lust that had been thrumming through her all week ramped up yet again.

This was ridiculous.

Nyree made the decision then and there to go after what she wanted. The whole flirting thing was fun and all, but she wanted more. She refused to spend the next seven weeks existing in this state of pent-up sexual frustration.

They were adults. Just because he was technically working for her, it didn't mean they couldn't take the time to explore the obvious attraction they'd both done such a horrible job of trying to fight. She knew exactly what she wanted, and the sooner she stopped beating around the bush, the better.

Nyree folded her arms over her chest and leaned back against her car door.

"Before we look at the chair and counter, I need to get a couple of things out on the table," she said. She took a deep breath. "First, the work on the house takes precedent over everything else. It *has* to be operational by the first week in April."

Dale's brow dipped with his confused frown. "We've covered this already, haven't we?"

"Yes, but I wanted to make sure it's understood."

"April 4th. The date is etched into my brain. In fact, I've mapped out a timetable that has me completing the work by the last weekend in March. As long as there are no huge surprises, the house will be ready in plenty of time."

"Good," Nyree said with a firm nod as she pushed away from the SUV. She walked over to where he stood, stopping a couple of feet in front of him. She squared her shoulders before she finally spoke. "I'm tired of playing this game we've been playing for the past week."

His frown deepened. "What game is that?"

"The game where we're both pretending that we don't want to rip each others' clothes off at the end of the day," she said.

She saw the way his chest expanded with the deep breath he sucked in.

"Ah, okay," he said. "*That* game."

"Yeah, *that* game."

He rubbed the back of his head. "So, uh, what do you suggest we do instead of playing that game?"

Her mouth curved up in a quick grin. "What do you normally do when you're attracted to someone?"

He stared at her with hooded eyes. Heat suffused her body with every second that passed.

"That's what I was hoping you'd say," she said.

His laugh was strained. "Are you sure about this, Nyree?"

"As long as things remain professional during work hours, I don't see why it would be a problem. Unless you don't—"

"Don't even think it," Dale said. He swallowed audibly. "I want. Damn, do I want."

He sauntered up to her and brushed the backs of his fingers along her bare arm. Goosebumps immediately formed on her skin.

"Why don't you show me the chair and counter, and then we can figure out what kind of things people who are attracted to each other do when they're together."

Now *she* was the one who had a hard time breathing.

Nyree collected as much air in her lungs as she could muster, then motioned for him to follow her to the shed behind the house. It's where they'd stored everything when they cleared out her aunt's beauty salon. Reesa had bought a lot of Hazel's supplies, but the chair and counter were two things Nyree hadn't been willing to part with.

"Here they are," Nyree said.

Dale walked around the bright green linoleum counter with the faded black splash mark, courtesy of the bottle of hair dye Nyree had knocked over when she worked reception in her aunt's shop after school. He ran his hand along the scuffed surface.

"I like the idea of including this," he said. "With the newness of everything that's being renovated, this will add some character."

"And it will be a wonderful tribute to my aunt," Nyree said. "So you think it can fit in the vestibule without crowding the space?"

"I don't think this will be too much of a problem. I'll take some measurements and see where—"

"What's *that* asshole doing here?"

Nyree turned to see her oldest brother, Desmond, standing in the shed's open doorway.

"Desmond Grant?" Dale asked, shock saturating his voice. "What the hell?" His head whipped around to Nyree. "Holy shit. Your last name—"

"Is Grant," Desmond said. "Same as mine. Now, what the hell are you doing around my little sister?"

Dale blew out a breath. "*Shiiit*," he said. "I can't believe I didn't put two and two together."

"I can," Desmond said. "Not many dumb jocks can do simple math."

"Would you get out of here?" Nyree pushed at Desmond's chest, but of course it made no difference. The big oaf didn't move even a centimeter.

She sensed a change in Dale the minute he recognized Desmond. Tension rolled off of him; his jaw was tight with it.

Nyree looked back and forth between the two men. "Hold on," she said. "How do you two know each other?"

Desmond hooked a thumb toward Dale. "This is the asshole who blindsided me during the homecoming game my senior year. Bastard broke my clavicle." Desmond rubbed his shoulder area. "But then someone busted up his knee while he was playing college ball." He smiled snidely at Dale. "That's called karma. She's a bitch, ain't she?"

"I didn't blindside you," Dale defended. "If you'd been paying attention to your assignment instead of trash talking, you would have seen me coming."

Desmond stuck his finger in Dale's face. "It was a bitch move and you know it, Chauvin."

"It was a clean hit," Dale countered, slapping Desmond's hand away.

Nyree stepped between the two of them, pushing at their heaving chests. "You're kidding me, right? You're both talking about something that happened years ago on a high school football field?"

"It was a clean hit," Dale said again.

"Bitch move," Desmond spat.

"Would you get out of here!" Nyree yelled at him.

"Not until he tells me why he's here," her brother said.

If it was anyone else standing before her, Nyree would feel ashamed at the devilish thrill that rushed through her, but her brother had been the biggest asshole lately. She would savor this.

She crossed her arms over her chest and smiled. "I hired Dale to do the renovations on the Whitmer House. He's been working there for nearly a week already."

Desmond's eyes widened as he shook his head with vehement disapproval.

"No way. Forget it," he said. "You don't need him to do a damn thing for you. Lance and I will take care of the house."

"I don't think so," Nyree said. She tipped her head to the side. "What did you tell me again? That my product line was just a little 'hobby'?" she said, making air quotes. "And that it's your way or the highway when it comes to renovating the house? And that I could wait until you were good and ready to start on it?" She pointed to the door. "Well, guess what? You can take the highway. I've got things covered here."

Desmond's nostrils flared. His gaze fluctuated from her to Dale before he cursed and turned for the door. Nyree followed, closing the door to the shed behind him.

She turned to find Dale standing with one hand behind his head, kneading his neck.

"So, you're Desmond and Lance Grant's little sister."

"Is that a problem?" Nyree asked.

His brow arched. "You really have to ask that after what just went down in here?"

Nyree put her hands up. "Okay, before you go any further, let's get one thing straight. Neither Desmond nor Lance have any say whatsoever over any aspect of my life." She motioned up and down her body. "What you see standing in front of you is a grown woman. Don't think for even a second that I answer to those two."

"Something tells me your brothers don't see it that way." He pitched his head toward the door. "So, should I expect Lance to show up soon?"

"Probably," Nyree said. "It's almost dinner time. I'm sure he'll be here in a few minutes, because he's incapable of cooking for himself like an adult."

"Thanks for the dinner invitation, but it's probably better if I'm gone by then," he said.

She folded her arms over her chest. "So, what's the deal between you and my brothers?"

Dale shook his head. "There's just some really bad blood there."

"I assume you played for the Mustangs?"

He nodded.

"I'm not the biggest football fan, but even I know that the rivalry between the Maplesville Mustangs and the St. Pierre Pirates goes back a long time. I remember this huge fight during Lance's senior year. The refs called the game before halftime."

"Your brother threw the first punch," Dale argued.

Nyree's eyes went wide. "That was *you*?"

Dale rubbed the back of his head again. "Yeah, that was me. I guess Lance called himself getting back at me for that hit against Desmond the year before." He looked up. "How do you remember that fight? Were you at the game?"

"Yeah. I was a freshman the year Lance graduated from high school. Thank God we only had one year together."

Dale grinned. "Overprotective much?"

She rolled her eyes. "If you only knew. I wouldn't have had a social life at all if I'd had to go through my entire high school career with Lance glaring at every boy that so much as looked at me."

"Can't say I blame them," Dale said. "If you were my little sister —"

Nyree shushed him with a finger to his lips. "Don't even say the words."

His lips stretched into a smile underneath her finger, which remained on his mouth. "Probably better that I don't think of you that way," he said.

His cellphone rang, startling them both.

Dale pulled it from his pocket and glanced at the screen, but instead of answering the phone, he pressed the red decline button and shoved it in his pocket.

"I have to be somewhere," he said. "Actually, I should have been there five minutes ago."

A thought occurred to her. Nyree gestured to the pocket where he'd put his phone. "I just realize that I never asked you this, but is there a girlfriend in the picture? You can be straight with me."

He shook his head. "There's no girlfriend."

His admission made her feel ridiculously happy. "Good," she said with a smile.

Dale blew out an exasperated breath. "There's no girlfriend, but—"

"Don't say it." She could tell what he was thinking. Reluctance traced across his features. "Don't even think it," Nyree said, repeating the words he'd said to her not even twenty minutes ago.

Dale tilted his head back and kneaded the bridge of his nose. He said it anyway. "Me and you…it probably isn't a good idea."

"Neither is eating an entire pan of brownies, but I did that last week and I don't regret a single crumb," she said. "I'm not saying we have to dive into anything serious. What's wrong with the two of us having coffee or dinner while talking about something other than the house renovations?"

She closed the distance between them and wrapped her fingers around his wrists. "Are you attracted to me?"

"Do you really have to ask that question?"

"Apparently," she answered.

He blew out another breath. "Yes. I am attracted to you. I'm absurdly attracted to you."

"I don't think it's absurd at all, because I feel the same way." She squeezed his hands. "We can start slow. Okay?"

He nodded, a small smile traveling across his lips. "Yeah, okay."

Nyree could barely contain the giddiness coursing through her. The urge to stand up on her tiptoes and kiss him slammed into her, but she was afraid he'd freak out. Instead, she just smiled like a delighted loon while still holding onto his hands.

The door to the shed opened and Desmond poked his head in. "You're still here? Don't you have a house?"

Dale tried to pull his hands away, but Nyree tightened her grip. She looked at her brother. "Leave," she said.

"Mama said the lasagna is ready," Desmond said. He pointed to Dale. "He's not eating dinner here."

"He is if he wants to," Nyree said.

"Thanks, but I have to get going," Dale reminded her. He gently slipped his hands from her grip.

Desmond snorted as he closed the door.

"Don't let Desmond get to you," Nyree said.

"Your brothers have been pains in my ass since high school," Dale said. "This is just par for the course."

"I have to admit, knowing that it pisses Desmond off to have you working for me is a bonus I hadn't expected."

Dale's deep chuckle reverberated around the small shed. "Happy I could be of service." He ran the back of his fingers along her arm in a gentle caress. Goosebumps immediately populated her skin. "I really need to get going," he said.

"And I need to get through dinner so I can get back to painting baseboards."

"Are you sleeping at Whitmer House?"

She nodded. "Now that I've moved my old futon there I'll probably split my nights between my apartment and the house."

"Remember, I plan to work there full-time starting tomorrow, so don't be alarmed when I'm knocking on the door at five a.m."

"You are *not* showing up at five a.m.," Nyree said.

"Hey, you're the one who wants the house to be done in less than two months."

"Fine," she said. "But don't be surprised when I'm still wearing my pajamas."

He tipped his head back and let out a weary sigh.

"What's wrong?" Nyree asked.

"You just ruined my fantasy. All this time I was hoping you didn't wear any pajamas."

Nyree burst out laughing. She stood on her tiptoes and brought her lips to his ear.

"Just remember, everything's negotiable."

Dale climbed into his truck but he didn't start the ignition. Instead, he thumped his forehead onto the steering wheel, cursing the universe and everything in it.

Desmond and Lance Grant?

Seriously?

Of the billions of men around the world, Nyree's older brothers just *had* to be Desmond and Lance, two of the biggest dicks on the planet. The Grant boys were known as "Double Trouble" back in their high school football days. The name fit. They *were* trouble.

And they were Nyree's brothers.

"Shit," Dale whispered.

That revelation sealed it for him. As much as he wanted it to happen, there wasn't even the remote possibility of he and Nyree getting together. It was a dicey proposition from the start and now there was just no way.

She may be cute as hell, and the way those medical scrubs hugged her ass had him planning out the wet dream he'd have tonight, but it wasn't worth the drama of dealing with the Grant boys. Just seeing Desmond again resurrected thoughts of a time that Dale had fought hard to put behind him. A time in his life that he now looked back on with regret.

He had *so* damn many regrets. Over what he'd allowed other people to do to him back then. Over the way he'd allowed himself to be used and then tossed away like a washed up rag doll once he could no longer be of use on the football field.

Dale banged his fist against the steering wheel.

He couldn't go there. Not right now. He didn't have the time.

—

He needed to be there for Sam, and the last thing his friend needed was Dale coming over feeling all salty over past disappointments.

Finally, he started up the truck and backed out of the driveway. As he drove toward Highway 421, a black Mustang rolled past him. Lance Grant sat behind the wheel.

Dale shook his head. He hadn't seen the Grant boys for months. Not since he ran into them back at The Corral, when a drunken Sam nearly got his ass kicked for trash talking with them. Yet here he was, seeing both Desmond and Lance in the span of twenty minutes.

No, he did not need this kind of drama in his life.

Twenty minutes later, he parked his pickup in an open space in front of Sam's apartment complex. Dale had considered moving into one of these newer places that had come up in the last couple of years, but he was comfortable in the little one-bedroom shotgun he rented in an older part of Maplesville. Sure, he had to drive a little farther to pick up a fast food burger or buy groceries, but it was an inconvenience he'd learned to live with.

He entered Sam's apartment and instantly felt the pall that had settled over the place. No words were said, only a short nod between him, Ian, and Sam, who sat slumped on the sofa, a can of ginger ale in his hand.

A few months ago Sam would have been drinking a beer, or even a glass of hard liquor.

They'd all had their first taste of alcohol back in high school, but it had never been anything to get worked up about. A beer while watching the NFL on Sunday, maybe toasting each other with a shot of whiskey when one of them had good news to share.

However, once Sam's dad was diagnosed with ALS, their friend's drinking went from occasional to daily. And as his dad's illness progressed, so did Sam's drinking. A few months ago, Dale and Ian decided an intervention was in order.

So far, so good.

There were times when Dale still felt as if Sam was teetering too close to the edge, but he was no longer on the brink of losing control. Now that they'd all come to terms with the fact that Charlie Stewart's death was imminent, they were all figuring out their own ways of dealing with it. One of those ways was just being together.

Dale grabbed a Pepsi from the fridge and went over to the sofa, taking a seat on the opposite end from Sam. A basketball game was on the TV, but not being a huge fan, Dale didn't pay much attention to the various teams outside of the New Orleans franchise.

As time ticked by, Dale wished he could say that the silence was comfortable, but it wasn't. Tonight was different. Ian had called him on his way from St. Pierre and filled Dale in on the decision Sam and his mom had made to transfer

Charlie to a hospice facility. It was another significant step on the road to saying goodbye. The reality of what was happening just a few miles down the road at Sam's parents' house filled the space.

Another ten uneasy minutes crawled by before Sam picked up the remote and lowered the volume on the game.

"Alright, this is depressing the shit out of me. Talk," Sam said. He tossed the remote on the sofa cushion between them and turned to Dale. "Ian said you left Harding to work on some old house?"

Dale took a sip of his drink, then set it next to a bowl of popcorn that sat on one of the milk crates that stood in for a coffee table.

"I haven't left Harding permanently," he said. "One of Vanessa's clients was desperate for a contractor, but couldn't find one who could do the job by her deadline. I'm helping her to renovate the old Whitmer place on Silver Oak." He gave them a brief overview of what Nyree planned to do with the house, before dropping the bomb on them. "But get this, she's Desmond and Lance Grant's younger sister."

"Oh, shit!" Ian burst out laughing. "I haven't seen those two since that night at The Corral."

Sam huffed. "I ran into Lance at a club in New Orleans a few weeks ago. He was trying to run game on this girl that was way out of his league. Craziest part? She fell for it. Who would have thought Shrek would get some play?"

Dale didn't ask what his friend was doing at a club. He'd have to trust that Sam was capable of making smart choices from now on.

"Well," he continued. "Nyree sure as hell doesn't take after him. Hard to believe she's even related to those two."

"Oh yeah?" Sam asked, twisting around on the sofa to face Dale. "So, what's she like?"

"What are we? Thirteen?"

"C'mon, man," Sam droned. "Don't start holding back on us now."

What was the point in remaining tight lipped? Ian and Sam already knew every damn thing about him. Did it really matter if they knew he had it bad for his two biggest enemies' younger sister?

"I'm not holding anything back, because nothing happened and nothing will happen." God, it pained him to say that. Dale looked over at his two friends. "I gotta admit, she's hot as hell."

"How hot?" Ian asked.

"On a scale of poblano to habanero," Sam said. Dale rolled his eyes at the mention of his friend's ludicrous chili-pepper scale. "Come on, man. What is she? Ancho? Serrano?"

"Ghost pepper," Dale answered.

"Bullshit," his friends both said at the same time.

Dale took another sip from his soda can. "I swear," he said. "Turns out she was only a freshman at St. Pierre High back when we were seniors at Maplesville."

"Desmond Grant will go ballistic if you try to get with his little sister," Sam said.

"I won't try to get with her, but it doesn't have a damn thing to do with whether or not Desmond approves," Dale said. He wanted to get that straight, for both his friends and for himself.

Okay, fine. For a few moments there he'd allowed himself to consider the possibility of starting something with Nyree, but Dale knew it wasn't a good idea even before her brothers came into the picture. He would heed Vanessa's warning about the risks involved in hooking up with someone you're doing business with. He'd done enough things in his life that he eventually regretted. He didn't want to add to the list.

"I have a job to do for her," Dale continued. "That's what I need to concentrate on. This renovation project is the perfect opportunity to jumpstart my own general contractor business."

"You're still talking about that, man?" Sam asked. "What about that kid you're coaching? Now *that's* what you should concentrate on."

Dale heaved an exhausted breath. "Don't start with that again," he said. "This training thing with Kendrick is just a one-time gig."

"How is the training going?" Ian asked.

"We've only had four sessions, but so far I'm impressed. I meet with him again tomorrow," Dale said. "There's only a couple of months before spring training starts, and his dad is sending him to this football camp somewhere up north. He wants him to be — and I quote — 'better than any other linebacker in the country'."

"From what you've said about him, his dad sounds like a dick."

"His dad *is* a dick, but Kendrick isn't a bad kid. And, to be honest, he has the potential to be one of the best in the country. The kid's instincts on the field are on point. We just need to work on his concentration."

"Dude, you need to do this full-time," Ian said. "The staff at Maplesville High would hire you as an assistant coach in a minute. I'm tired of telling you this."

And Dale was tired of hearing it. His friends had been on his back for well over a year about coaching at their old high school, ever since one of the long-time assistant coaches left to teach at a high school in Baton Rouge. Once he started working with Kendrick, both Sam and Ian had jumped on that bandwagon. If he didn't want to coach full time, both thought he should launch his own football-training business.

Dale would never admit it to his friends, but he'd been tempted. With the competition for spots on high school and collegiate teams getting tougher, there was a growing market for one-on-one private instructors.

When Lowell Robertson first approached him about tutoring Kendrick in the middle linebacker position, Dale hadn't been sure how to respond. After his career-ending injury in the

Senior Bowl in college, which took away all dreams of playing in the NFL and changed the course of his life, Dale had walked away from football. It had taken him two years before he could even bring himself to watch a game on television. But once he welcomed football back into his life, he'd quickly fallen back in love with the game.

Coaching would be like a dream come true for him. There was something seductive about the game that called to him.

Back when he was in high school, he never just played the game. He'd studied it. Lived it. He would spend hours going over plays in his head. He would workout in his backyard, using lawn furniture as opposing players, timing the quickness in which he could get past a defender.

Back then, football wasn't just a game to him. It was *everything*.

And therein lay his biggest problem.

Maybe if he had paid attention to something other than football, he would have recognized that the game could be snatched away from him in an instant. And he could have been better prepared for a life without it.

"Enough with me," Dale said, needing to put an end to this subject. He turned to Ian. "What about you? How was Las Vegas? You lose all your money at the blackjack table?"

"I didn't get a chance to even see the blackjack table," Ian said. "Sonny's cupcake baking competition took up most of our time."

"That's a good thing, because you suck at blackjack," Sam said.

Ian pitched an empty water bottle at his head.

"It's all good. The cupcake competition is the reason we went out there in the first place," he pointed out.

Ian's girlfriend, Madison White, was Maplesville's new star pastry chef. Sonny had arrived in town last year in her little VW Beetle, rocking a huge Afro and looking like someone who'd walked straight out of a Pam Grier movie from the 70s. She'd started out as Ian's tenant, living in the apartment above his garage. But that arrangement only lasted a few months. She'd moved from Ian's garage to his house, and was now helping him to raise his teenage sister, Kimmie.

"I'm sorry Sonny didn't win the grand prize," Dale said.

"She came in fifth, which is still pretty awesome," Ian said. "It was enough in prize money to cover the cost of the trip, and now she can say that she placed in a national baking contest. Sonny wasn't going out there to win it all. She just wanted to gain some name recognition."

"At least you two had a good time," Sam said.

Ian nodded and shrugged. "We also got married, so that's good."

Sam and Dale both stared for several

heartbeats before they simultaneously shouted, "What!"

Ian just sat there expressionless, as if he hadn't just dropped atomic bomb-size news on them.

"What?" he asked with another shrug. "We were going to do it eventually. We passed one of those wedding chapels on our way to the hotel when we first arrived and decided to pop in and get married."

"Dude, who does that?" Dale said.

"More people than you might think," Ian replied. "We had to wait almost an hour before it was our turn."

Sam burst out laughing. "I guess this calls for a toast." He held up his can of ginger ale. "To your bachelorhood going down in a blaze of glory."

"My bachelorhood was gone the minute I met Sonny," Ian said. "But I'll drink to a long and happy life with my beautiful wife."

Sam looked at Ian with total disgust. "Just go write greeting cards for a living."

Ian flipped him his middle finger as he grabbed a handful of popcorn from the bowl. He motioned for Sam to turn up the volume on the TV.

As Dale observed his two friends, he couldn't quell a rush of envy. Of the three of them, *he* was the one who always was supposed to have the brightest future. Everyone knew he would make it to the NFL. From the very first tackle he'd made during tryouts for the varsity team his freshman year of high school, it's all Dale had ever heard.

Fast forward a little over a decade later, and he felt like the biggest failure to come out of Maplesville.

Here was Ian, married to a beautiful woman, working a good job at the concrete plant and slowly building his own motorcycle repair business. And even though Sam had gone through a rough patch over the past year while coming to terms with his dad's illness, he was gradually getting his act together. Vanessa's real estate firm was thriving. Hell, Sonny was even making a name for herself with her cupcakes. It was sad that he could be jealous over cupcake-success, but damn if he wasn't.

It seemed as if everyone was on the fast track, while he was stagnant, working construction for someone else when he should, at the very least, have his own contractor business by now. If the Grant boys could do it, he sure as shit should be able to do the same.

Not to mention the way their little sister was straight up winning at life.

If he were being honest with himself, Dale had to admit that one of his biggest hang-ups with dating Nyree was envy over just how much she'd already accomplished even though she was three years younger than his own twenty-seven years. How in the hell had she achieved so much already?

He made a good living, but he wasn't capable of buying a huge property like the Whitmer House. Heck, he still rented the small house he lived in.

He needed to get his shit together.

Maybe this renovation job really would be the catalyst for the next phase of his life. Working construction might not be his first choice, but he was good at it and if he actually owned a piece of a business, at least it would feel as if he'd achieved something.

It was time he got off his ass and started making things happen.

And it was yet another reason why he should steer clear of any kind of romantic entanglements with his boss. He needed to stay focused on his goals—goals that had nothing to do with the bedroom.

Chapter Four

Nyree fixed the tail end of the funnel firmly into the bottle's mouth. It was the last of several dozen newly delivered bottles that sat on the kitchen counter in her cluttered her apartment. She'd been in the middle of boxing up more of her belongings when the deliveryman knocked on her door. It had been the death knell to packing. She still had weeks before she had to move everything into her rooms at the Whitmer House anyway; she could afford to sacrifice the afternoon.

Nyree poured the remaining drops of the rosemary and peppermint leave-in conditioner she'd mixed up yesterday, giving a fist pump when she realized she had just enough product to fill the bottle.

"Couldn't have turned out better if I'd planned it this way," Nyree said.

She capped the first bottle, but was too impatient to worry about the rest of them just yet. Leaving the others uncapped, she pulled a label from the roll that had arrived last week.

Her heartbeats reached insane levels as she affixed the pale pink oval to the frosted gray bottle she'd chosen for her hair care line. It took

Nyree a moment to catch her breath as she stared at the finished product. Seeing the *Naturally Nyree* logo on her creation…knowing it would soon be sold to the masses. Well, at least to the people in Maplesville and surrounding areas. But that was a lot more than just the handful of Reesa's customers who purchased her products now.

With a physical storefront and the online store, the potential to grow this into a skin and hair care empire was certainly within the realm of possibility. She just had to continue putting in the work. And if there was one thing Nyree had never shied away from, it was working hard for what she wanted. She'd put in more than her share of long days and sleepless nights coming up with the perfect recipes for her products. And just look what she had to show for it.

"I told you I would do it, Aunt Hazel," Nyree whispered.

She would *not* cry. She refused.

If her aunt were standing here right now, she would call Nyree a crybaby and warn her not to sling snot all over her shirt. But Nyree couldn't staunch the tidal wave of emotion that suddenly overwhelmed her.

She had always looked up to her mother's younger sister, and wanted to be just like her. She'd spent hours after school and on the weekends hanging around Hazel's salon, soaking in the unique camaraderie between the women getting their hair done, waiting for the day when she could step into that role of stylists, just like her aunt.

Nyree could still recall the intense hurt she felt when her aunt refused to teach her how to style hair—especially after Hazel took Reesa under her wing. It wasn't until her aunt explained *why* she wouldn't teach her that Nyree finally began to understand just how much Hazel believed in *her*. She told Nyree that she wanted to see her sitting behind a desk in a college classroom, not standing on her feet all day behind a salon chair.

If she closed her eyes and dug deep enough into her memory, Nyree could remember just how it felt when Hazel wrapped her arms around her and refused to let go after hearing that Nyree had earned a full-ride scholarship to Dillard University. Her aunt told her that it was one of the proudest days of her life. Nyree only wished she'd been healthy enough to see her walk across the stage when she earned her degree, but by then Hazel's body was so riddled with cancer that she was barely able to move.

Nyree closed her eyes and pulled in a deep, cleansing breath, willing the tears to remain at bay.

There would be no more tears when she thought about her aunt. Her mission these days was to keep Hazel's memory alive through the legacy she'd left behind. Every jar of *Naturally Nyree* product would be a tribute to Hazel, with a percentage of the proceeds going to the Cancer

Treatment Center at the hospital in Slidell that
took care of her aunt in her final days.

Nyree capped the remaining bottles of leave-
in conditioner and affixed the labels to them.
Once that was finished, she put her hands on her
hips and looked around her living room and
kitchen, which were both cluttered with packing
boxes, mixing bowls, blocks of pure Shea butter,
and too many bottles of essential oils to count.

She had two choices: clean up around here
or don't. She picked don't.

It would just look this way in a couple of
days when she whipped up the body butter and
cuticle cream she planned on making this
weekend. Besides, she had more important
things to do with her time than to worry about
the mess in her apartment.

Like worrying about the mess at Whitmer
House.

Nyree wanted to cry when she thought
about how much work remained, yet she
couldn't help but marvel at what Dale had been
able to accomplish over these past three weeks.

Especially this last week, when she'd only
managed to spend a few hours pitching in. She'd
planned to spend most of her time at the
Whitmer House, having saved up enough
vacation time to work only two shifts a week for
the next several months. But after a coworker's
entire family came down with a late-season flu,
Nyree found herself working in the lab all week.

Of course, it was probably for the best that

she had some time away from Dale after the way he'd flaked on her. She'd been so sure that they were on the same page after they left her grandmother's shed a couple of weeks ago, but the following day he'd said that he didn't think it was a good idea to see each other.

At first Nyree told herself to just let it go. She couldn't force him to do something he didn't want to do. He thought it best they remain professional, despite the torrential dose of chemistry that bubbled up between them whenever they came in contact? Fine. She'd have to live with it.

Then she'd come to her senses.

Dale had been on board until he found out who her brothers were. There was no way Nyree would allow those two meatheads to be the reason she and Dale didn't get a chance to explore the white-hot attraction that singed the air between them.

Dale thought his declaration a couple of weeks ago was the end of it, but he'd underestimated her. Because once she set her mind out to accomplish something, she didn't stop until she reached her goal.

In this case, her goal was Dale Chauvin.

A text message came through on her phone just as the alert system Desmond had installed above her front door dinged, indicating that someone was approaching. Nyree pulled up the text as she made her way to the door.

She stopped mid-step as she read the text

from Lance.

I'm on my way up. Let me in.

There was a knock at the door.

"Come on, Nyree. Open up," her brother called.

Nyree let out a frustrated sigh as she unlocked the door and opened it for him. "What are you doing here?" she asked as Lance stood just outside the door. When he didn't enter, she asked, "Are you waiting for an invitation to come inside?"

"From the way you've been acting lately, I don't know if I'm welcome," he said.

"Stop being such a drama queen." She pushed the door open and walked back to the kitchen. "What are you even doing in this part of town right now?" she asked over her shoulder.

"This," he said. "I came here to talk to you. I want to help you with the house."

Nyree rested her hip against the kitchen cabinet and folded her arms over her chest. "Really? Did you have this change of heart after you found out I hired Dale Chauvin to do the job?"

"I don't give a crap about Chauvin. I promised you I'd work on the house for you. You should have come to me instead of just going through Desmond."

"He's the one who makes the schedule for Grant Construction."

"I don't care about what is and what isn't a Grant Construction job, either. I told you I'd help you out, now let me," Lance said.

Nyree could hear the frustration and regret in his voice. She hated that her relationship with her brothers was so complicated, but her own resentment toward them had built up so much over the years that it was often hard to see past it. Just because Lance had suddenly suffered a bout of guilt over leaving her in the lurch again, did that mean she should automatically forgive him and accept his help with a smile?

Not today.

"Thanks, but no thanks," Nyree said.

The pain that flashed across his handsome face nearly made her take back her words. But she excelled at being stubborn, so instead of apologizing, as she should have, she walked back to the front door and opened it. Lance stood in the kitchen for several long moments, staring at her with those amber eyes that were so much like her own.

Nyree fought the urge to smooth things over. She was always the one expected to be the bigger person when it came to her two brothers. She'd spent her life watching their needs get catered to by her mother and grandmother, feeling compelled to do the same because everything had always been about Desmond and Lance.

Well, it was about her this time. She didn't need their help. When Any Way You Want It Salon and Spa opened its doors, she could be proud of what she'd been able to accomplish without them.

Lance finally moved, walking to where she stood. He stopped just outside the door. "You sure about this?" he asked.

"See you at dinner on Sunday," she said in a saccharine voice, just because she knew it would irritate him.

Okay, fine. So she could be both stubborn *and* petty. She really needed to work on that.

When she closed the door behind him, Nyree felt another twinge of guilt, but she managed to shake it off. Lance's hurt feelings were not her problem.

She went over to the fridge and grabbed the sliced smoked turkey breast she'd picked up from the deli on her way from work a couple of hours ago, along with a loaf of 12-grain bread. She packed the sandwiches, a couple bags of potato chips and two apples into the refrigerated bag she'd gotten for participating in last year's walk-a-thon at work.

Twenty-five minutes later, Nyree pulled in behind Dale's pickup in the driveway at Whitmer House. It was funny that she still thought of it as Whitmer House, even though she now owned it.

"The bank owns the bulk of it," Nyree reminded herself. And they would own it for many, many years to come.

Unless the *Naturally Nyree* line took off and made her millions, of course. It was a long-shot, but longer shots had happened for others. Why not her?

Nyree grabbed the bag with the sandwiches and climbed out of her SUV. A light mist had begun to fall on her way over from St. Pierre. She scampered up the walkway and entered the house through the front door. She was greeted by the whirl of a table saw, and the sexiest naked back she'd ever seen in her life. Her mouth felt as if she'd swallowed a handful of the sawdust flying through the air.

If not for the power tool's buzzing and the music pouring from the speaker connected to Dale's cellphone, Nyree was certain he would have heard her pulse's erratic thumping.

God, but he looked good. She'd missed seeing him this week. Missed him so much more than she ever thought she could miss someone who was, technically, just an employee.

His choice, not hers.

He'd stubbornly stuck to his guns regarding the two of them not getting involved, but the sight of those muscles bunching underneath his sweat-slicked skin had her once again thinking of ways to change his mind.

She leaned against the new, unfinished wooden doorjamb he'd installed since she was last here, crossing her feet at the ankles and her arms over her chest. Nyree settled in, ready to enjoy this sexy display of flesh for as long as possible.

But with the spidey sense of a cock-blocking chaperone, Dale's head popped up and he turned his goggle-covered eyes on her. He immediately grabbed the t-shirt that draped off the edge of the sawhorse and pulled it over his head, covering up all that beautiful brown skin.

Damn him! She could have stood there for the next hour watching his muscles flex.

Dale picked up his cellphone and lowered the music, but he didn't turn it off. Nyree recognized the song. It was the latest by a local R&B artist from New Orleans who had been blowing up on social media lately.

She nodded toward the phone. "I didn't realize you were a fan. I just bought Simone's newest single on iTunes. She did one of those Beyoncé-style drops last night. No one even knew there was a new album in the works."

"I hadn't heard about a new album," he said. "I'll have to download it." He gestured to the padded cooler still hanging from her shoulder. "Please tell me there's food in there?"

"I made sandwiches."

The genuine smile that traced across his lips as he walked to her made her skin tingle.

"You must be psychic," he said. "I was just about to stop so I could grab something from that store around the corner."

"Not psychic, just used to taking care of my brothers and their friends. They used to spend hours outside playing basketball, and wouldn't come inside to eat unless my mom dragged them into the house." She motioned to the saw. "I can tell that's your version of shooting hoops."

He laughed. "Football's my sport, remember? And you have to admit that saw is a pretty sweet toy."

He reached for the bag, but Nyree pulled it away. She pointed to the small bathroom just off to the right of the parlor.

"It will gross me out if you eat this sandwich with all that dust on you. At least wash your hands."

"I've been inhaling dust on construction sites for the past five years. Washing my hands won't do me much good."

She just continued to stare at him.

"Fine," he said in the same tortured voice her brothers would use when she interrupted their basketball games. Nyree couldn't help but laugh.

As he washed up, she used a towel to sweep as much of the saw dust from the floor as she could, then used the soft-sided lunch bag as a placemat, setting the sandwiches and fruit on it so they wouldn't get dirty. She openly ogled Dale as he walked back toward her. She wondered if he maintained that body strictly through working construction or if, like her older brothers, he spent enough time in the gym to list it as a second residence on his taxes.

He dropped down to the floor with a slight grimace. "Old football injury," he said.

He sat with one knee bent, his arm resting on top of it. He looked as if he was posing for the cover of a romance novel.

Well, maybe if he took the shirt off again.

"I think you may have a problem with your pipes," Dale said.

"Huh?" Had she heard him right? She'd been so mesmerized by the way his worn jeans stretched over his thigh that she couldn't be sure. "What about my pipes?"

He gestured toward the bathroom. "It's the second time I could hear rattling while washing my hands."

Ah, *those* pipes!

"What's going on with them?"

"Not sure," he said. "I looked for rotting when I tied in the plumbing for the shampoo stations, but that was only a small section. You never know what's lurking in the walls, especially in an old house like this one that hasn't had anyone living in it for a while."

"How much will this set us back—time wise—to look at all the pipes?"

"It won't take long to run some tests on the pipes," Dale said. "But if we find out that they're rotted, you're looking at weeks."

Nyree dropped her head back and sighed up at the ceiling. "Would it be foolish of me to take my chances? I don't have the time or the money to redo all the pipes."

Dale put his hands up. "It's your call," he said, taking the sandwich she'd handed him. He unwrapped it, picked up one half, and bit off almost the entire thing in one bite. "You know what I've been trying to figure out?" he said after swallowing. "How I didn't realize Desmond and Lance even had a sister."

"I'm not all that surprised that you'd never heard about me," she said. "It's always been about Desmond and Lance. The big football stars," Nyree said. She could hear the resentment in her voice and mentally cursed herself for it. "Forgive me," she said. "But I hate football."

Dale gasped with exaggerated shock. "Just stab me in the heart, why don't you?"

Nyree couldn't help but laugh at his antics.

"Sorry," she said. "You can blame Desmond and Lance. Back when I was younger, their football took precedence over everything." She popped open her bag of salt and vinegar chips. "My mom would drag me to their Pop Warner games, and then in high school everything was about making it to the state championship." She flicked her wrist in a dismissive wave. "People take it too seriously around here if you asked me."

"High school sports is like a religion here, and football is god."

"So, what does that make the rivalry between the Pirates and the Mustangs? Easter Sunday?"

"Easter, Christmas, and every other big holiday you can think of, all wrapped up into one."

"I remember back in those days when you

and my brothers played. That rivalry was crazy."

"The rivalry has always been crazy. Back in those days it was insane."

"Do you remember the cheating scandal? Someone called Coach Watson out for having a tape recorder in the opposing team's locker rooms at St. Pierre."

Dale, who'd just taken another bite of his sandwich, pointed to his chest.

Nyree's eyes went wide. "Wait! You?"

He chewed for a few seconds more, then swallowed. "Me," he answered. "Well, it was my coach who brought the charge to the Louisiana High School Sports Commission, but I was the one who alerted him to the recorder."

"Oh, my goodness. No wonder Desmond and Lance hate you."

"Yeah, I had a pretty big hand in ruining their high school football legacies."

"How did you find out about the cheating?"

He gulped down half the bottle of water, then wiped his mouth with the back of his hand, leaving a trace of dust. Nyree reached over and brushed it off his cheek with her thumb. Their eyes caught and held as she perched on her knees in front of him.

"Sawdust," she said. "You must have missed a spot when you washed up."

His mouth lifted in a too-sexy-for-her-to-handle grin. "Thanks."

Would it be too obvious if she pretended to

fall forward and landed on his chest? Probably so. The question was, did she care?

"Anyway," Dale continued. "The cheating scandal."

"Yes," Nyree said. She sat back down on her side of the impromptu picnic setup and managed not to kick and scream like a toddler who couldn't get her way. "So, how did you take down Coach Watson?"

"I had this pre-game ritual where I would go off by myself to clear my head. I was pacing back and forth in the locker room when I found the recorder wedged between two benches."

"Coach Watson was suspended for the rest of the season after that. He almost lost his job, didn't he?" Nyree popped another potato chip in her mouth and sucked the salt from her fingers.

Dale's gaze zeroed in on her lips. "Uh, yeah," he said.

Nyree was tempted to draw her fingers back into her mouth, and lick them up and down, but Dale tore his eyes away before she could.

Dammit. She should have been quicker.

"Watson nearly lost his job," he continued. "But everybody in St. Pierre rallied around him."

"I remember when that happened," Nyree said, resignedly returning to their conversation. "They had that big meeting in the gymnasium and two of the teachers almost got into a fight. You caused all kinds of headaches when you found that recorder. I thought it was awesome."

"Not everyone agrees with you." He grimaced. "That next year—my senior year—was one of the roughest I've ever been through on the football field. Even though Coach Watson was cheating against all the Pirates' opponents, not just the Mustangs, some people were upset that the LHSSC came down on him. I violated a code by turning him in. And, let's face it, no one likes a snitch."

Nyree sobered. "You became a target."

He nodded. "It seemed as if every player was gunning for me in every game that year, but the one against the Pirates was the worst. I've never been hit as hard as I was during that game."

Nyree rolled her eyes. "Let me guess. Lance was ruthless."

"Oh, yeah," Dale said. He rubbed his shoulder. "I can feel those hits as if they happened yesterday."

"As I remember it, Desmond and Lance both hated you mainly because you were the player from this area who was granted the top NFL prospect crown back when you all were in high school."

His huff of laughter didn't hold an ounce of humor. "Funny how quickly that crown can get knocked off."

"Wait. The hit from Lance isn't the reason you're not playing in the NFL, is it?

He shook his head. "No, that happened in the Senior Bowl." Tension flowed from him. She could see it in the tightness of his jaw. "The craziest part is that I didn't even have to play in the game. The Senior Bowl is basically for those players who are still trying to land a spot on an NFL team. It's a way to showcase your talents to scouts."

"You didn't need to show anyone your football skills?"

"I had four teams seriously vying for me. I was predicted to go in the top ten of the NFL draft that year. I didn't need to play in the Senior Bowl. But I *wanted* to. I loved playing college ball, and I'd heard over and over again how it's a totally different game once you get to the NFL. I just wanted to experience one last time what it felt like to play on the college level."

Nyree couldn't help but ache for him. She sensed how difficult it was for him to even talk about it, but she wanted to know more. Despite all the hours they'd spent together over the past few weeks, this was the first conversation of true substance they'd shared. She wasn't ready to see it come to an end.

Keeping her voice gentle, Nyree asked, "What happened? The injury, I mean."

He kept his gaze on the wall, just over her shoulder. "It was the last play of the first half of the game. I got blindsided and went down hard. I tore all four ligaments in my knee and dislocated my kneecap."

"Goodness," Nyree said, covering his hand with her own. "What about surgery?"

"I had several, but it's not the kind of injury you can come back from." He shrugged. "There were a couple of teams who showed some interest. They brought me out to their facilities, had me workout for them, but I knew better than to think I'd ever get to play a single down of professional football. I also suffered my third concussion in that game. That's something that you just never fully recover from, no matter what anyone says."

Nyree sucked in a deep breath and blew it out with an uneasy sigh. "That's the one thing I feared the most back when Desmond and Lance both played. As much as I resented all the attention they used to get because they played football, I was still so afraid of them getting hurt."

"It's a violent sport, but around here we're brought up to love it from birth. And I did," Dale said. "The game itself, when it's pure and not muddied with all the politics and bullshit that surrounds it, is one of the best things in the world."

"You still love it," Nyree said. "I can hear it in your voice."

"I do," he admitted. "But my football days are behind me. I'm good with that. You just have to accept what life throws at you and do your best to keep moving." His mouth quirked in a half-smile. "It would be nice if someone could tell that to Desmond. It's pretty ridiculous that he's still holding onto a grudge from high school."

"My brothers were both meatheads back then." She tipped her head to the side. "Actually, they're still meatheads, but, believe it or not, they've gotten slightly better over the years. At least they wouldn't hit you now."

"I don't know about that." Dale lowered his eyes to her chest. "If they knew I was sitting here trying not to look down your shirt, they would."

An infusion of heat flooded her bloodstream. Nyree leaned forward so that the material gaped even more.

"My brothers have no say in who I let look down my shirt."

"Did you wear it on purpose?" he asked.

"How calculating do you think I am?" she said with mock affront, though she couldn't hide her grin.

Dale balled up the plastic wrap the sandwiches were wrapped in and tossed it toward the pile of sawdust she'd swept up before they sat to eat.

"You have to admit you've been pretty direct when it comes to...well...this," he said, motioning between the two of them.

"Yes, I have been," Nyree agreed as she packed away the remnants of their meal. "Which is why I find it funny that you think I'd resort to games. If I wanted you to see what's under my shirt, I would just show you."

"Please don't," he said, his voice strained. "This is hard enough as it is."

She threw her hands up in frustration. "If this is so hard for you, why are you fighting it? I know this attraction isn't one-sided, Dale. You seemed interested until you discovered who my brothers were." She tilted her head to the side. "Or was I reading you wrong? "

He locked eyes with her. "No, you weren't."

"So why are you acting so damn skittish now?"

His forehead wrinkled. "Skittish? Who even uses that word?"

"Don't change the subject."

"I'm not changing the subject," he said. "But you need to understand that just because I'm attracted to you to the point that I can hardly think straight, it doesn't change anything."

She smiled at him as she leaned forward, making sure her shirt gaped far more than it previously had. "Actually, it does. It changes everything."

A pained look traced across his face. "Nyree—"

"If you think for a second that I'm going to let some stupid football rivalry from years ago come between what we could have, you're as big a meathead as my silly brothers."

His exasperated groan echoed around the cavernous room. "C'mon, Nyree. You know this isn't a good idea."

"Why not? Give me one reason." She held up her hand. "And your answer cannot have anything to do with Desmond or Lance. And none of that 'it isn't professional' crap, either. Oh, and don't even try to say that you don't want it, because nothing would bring me more pleasure than proving you wrong." Her gaze dropped to his lap. "I have my ways."

His Adam's apple bobbed with his pronounced swallow.

"So?" Nyree raised her brow. "What's your reason?"

"I, uh, I need some time to think about it."

"Wrong answer."

Dale rubbed the back of his neck. "It's just not a good idea, Nyree."

"I disagree." She waited for his rebuttal, but he remained silent. "Well, it looks as if we've arrived at an impasse. We both want different things."

"I never said I didn't want it," he said quickly. "I just said it wasn't a good idea."

A wicked grin curled up the edge of Nyree's lips. "Admitting that you want something to happen between us isn't the best way to get me to stop asking for it, Dale." She crawled up to him on all fours. She could tell how affected he was by the way his breathing slowed.

"You may want to give up this argument. You're going to lose. And, just so you know, I'm a pretty obnoxious winner. When you lose, I'm going to take great pleasure in rubbing it in."

Chapter Five

Dale stood with his legs braced apart and his arms crossed over his chest as he studied Kendrick's form. He watched the teen move from one apparatus to the next, executing the moves they'd practiced over the past two months with a precision that had Dale's chest puffing with pride. He'd earned the right to the satisfaction currently flowing through him. Kendrick's command over the middle linebacker position had grown by leaps and bounds since their first session.

What if he really *could* coach football?

Dale cursed the thought for even popping into his head. Whenever that happened he usually swatted it away, and cursed Sam and Ian for putting the suggestion there in the first place. The idea of coaching football on the high school level was way too seductive.

As he continued to watch Kendrick, it suddenly occurred to Dale how much he himself must resemble his old high school football coach. He could picture the old man standing in this same pose, the bill of that dusty maroon and white Maplesville Mustangs baseball cap pulled down low on his brow.

Damn, but he wished he could make this happen. Something about it felt so right.

But coaching at the high school level wasn't in the cards for him, and he damn well knew it.

For one thing, he needed a degree to become a high school coach, and the business degree he currently held wasn't worth shit. Dale would rather walk off three-story scaffolding than admit to his family that the degree he'd "earned" was useless.

That's why he needed to stick to construction. He didn't need a degree to swing a hammer.

But maybe he *could* make it work, at least in some way. Take what he was doing right now. Coaching full time may not be in the cards for him, but working as a one-on-one instructor was a pretty good substitute. He could learn to love tutoring just as much as he knew he'd love being an actual coach.

"Shit," Dale cursed underneath his breath. He would drive himself crazy going back and forth the way he had over this, lamenting about things that just weren't meant to be.

A late model Ford Focus pulled into the graveled parking lot just to the left of the park where he and Kendrick practiced. A teen who looked to be about the same age as Kendrick got out of the car and jogged to them.

"Can I have a minute?" Kendrick asked. "I need to handle this."

Dale's brow hitched in suspicion as he watched the other kid hand Kendrick a flash drive.

"Here you go," the boy said.

"It's five pages long, right?" Kendrick asked. "Mr. Dugas said the paper had to be five pages."

"It's four and a half."

"Good enough," Kendrick said. The two clasped hands and went in for a half hug. "Thanks, man." He held up the flash drive. "And you were right, this is better than emailing. Less of a paper trail."

The boy nodded toward Dale before heading back to his car.

Dale waited until he pulled off before he turned to Kendrick and asked, "What was that about?"

"Nothing. Just a friend helping me out."

His eyes narrowed as he regarded Kendrick. "Do you have someone else doing your homework for you?"

The boy laughed, waving off Dale's question. "Don't give me a hard time, man. You know how this is. I spend all my time training and conditioning. Something has to take a backseat, as long as it's not football."

"Football season is over," Dale said. "Although that shouldn't matter one way or the other. Your first priority should be class."

"Football season is never over," Kendrick said.

Dale would bet money the kid had heard

those same words from his father.

Kendrick tucked the flash drive in the pocket of his workout shorts. "Don't worry about what you just saw here. I've got this under control."

A sickening feeling started to settle in Dale's gut.

It was like déjà vu. He saw his high school and college self in the boy's every shrug. Dale could remember the way his fellow classmates clamored to do his homework for him — usually at the urging of the teachers and coaches — so that Dale could concentrate on the game and help the team win championships. That was always the number one goal. Damn the cost — do whatever was necessary to win.

Except *he* was the one now paying the price for it.

The cost was four wasted years in college when he should have been learning something. Instead, all he had to show for his time was a useless degree he hadn't earned.

An awful feeling filled Dale's gut as he remembered how much he used to relish all the attention. It took getting hurt to realize that *he* wasn't the one being revered. It was his skill on the football field. Once he no longer had that to offer, he was nothing.

"This isn't a joke, Kendrick," Dale said. "I know you're good at football. So was I. And that's why I know from experience that this football thing can be over in a blink of an eye."

He snapped his finger. "All it takes is one good hit, and your entire world changes. Don't sacrifice your education. I promise you, you're going to regret it."

If there was one thing Dale knew, it was the sting of regret. It lived inside of him. A haunting cloud that followed him constantly. Regret over how he'd allowed coaches and college boosters to make decisions that would affect him for the rest of his life. How he'd allowed so many to use him for their gain, while filling his head with everything he wanted to hear.

All that praise and esteem was a helluva drug, but once he lost it, the crash was unlike anything Dale could have ever imagined.

"I mean it, Kendrick," he told the teen again, but he could tell he wasn't getting through to him.

"It's all good, man," Kendrick said. "All that school stuff is handled." He looked down at his watch. "Aw, shit! I'm supposed to meet my girl in an hour. I need to go home and shower." He nudged his chin toward Dale. "I'll have that reaction time nailed down by the time we meet next week. Catch you later."

Dale responded with a reluctant nod. "I'll see you next week."

As he watched Kendrick jog toward his truck—a top-of-the-line double-cab pickup that no high school kid should be driving—Dale couldn't fight the nasty feeling that continued to fester in his gut.

He hated to see Kendrick get caught up in the mess he had. He'd seen it happen to too many. Not just to himself, but other kids who came out of the Deep South, where football reigned supreme. They were all kings of the field…until they were not.

As he picked up the orange cones he'd brought for running drills, Dale pondered what action, if any, he should take. Should he mention it to Lowell Robertson? Should he go directly to the school?

No. He knew better than to go to the school. The powers that be at Maplesville High knew exactly what went on back when he played ball. Dale wouldn't be surprised if it was one of Kendrick's coaches who'd recruited that other kid to write the term paper for him.

Some things just never changed.

"But they need to," Dale muttered.

If he were coaching high school, he would never allow the cheating that ran rampant in sports programs back when he played. And apparently still went on.

He pulled in a deep breath in an attempt to tamp down the annoyance that threatened to bubble over. Sooner or later he'd have to decide what route to take regarding Kendrick's cheating, but there was nothing he could do about it right that second.

Besides, there were other things on his plate that called for his attention. One thing in particular that Dale knew he would probably also live to regret.

Meeting up with Nyree was the exact opposite of what he should do tonight—or any night.

He shouldn't want to see her. The problem was that he *always* wanted to see her. He just didn't want to deal with the consequences, which usually included a painful hard-on and an eventual cold shower.

"You could tell her you got sick," he said to himself.

But there was no way he would do that, because despite the fact that he knew he should walk away from the temptation that was Nyree Grant, he didn't want to.

That's why when she'd texted him late last night, asking if he wanted to go see Simone Thibodaux in concert, Dale hadn't hesitated with his reply. And while he was looking forward to seeing the local R&B artist perform, the soulful Simone had nothing to do with the real reason why, after a grueling day of framing the new interior walls for the massage clinic at the Whitmer House and this afternoon's practice with Kendrick, his body was practically humming with excitement instead of exhaustion.

Dale threw the cones in the bed of his truck and slipped behind the wheel. He dropped his head onto the steering wheel and thumped it several times.

"Just say no. Just say no. Just say no."

If he were to sit here and come up with all

the reasons why he shouldn't meet with Nyree tonight, he'd be here until morning. The fact that he worked for her was bad enough, but even that didn't rank as high as knowing who her brothers were.

Yet, neither factored in as much as the sobering truth Dale couldn't deny.

He just wasn't good enough for her.

Not once had she even hinted that she felt that way, but just because she didn't see it yet, it didn't mean she wouldn't one day wake up and realize that she could do a lot better than a washed up college football star with a worthless degree and a bucketful of regrets.

How could she not see how mismatched they were? She had so much going for her, while he...well...didn't. He could have, but he'd squandered his chances a long time ago.

Yet, the understanding that Nyree was way out of his league didn't so much as enter his mind when he lay in his bed at night, thinking about her. Imagining what it would be like to have her petite body next to him, on top of him.

His groan reverberated around the truck cab.

He wasn't just asking for trouble. He was luring trouble over with a nice big juicy steak. Taunting it. Begging for it to follow him.

But he would have to contend with whatever consequences he faced, because he wanted her. He wanted to be with her.

Nyree was a breath of fresh air. A change

from the stagnant place he'd been stuck in for the past few years. He hadn't had a steady girlfriend since college, back when he'd foolishly thought himself in love.

Dale huffed out a humorless laugh.

His career-ending injury had taught him many lessons, but one of the hardest was learning how quickly people turned their backs on you when they deemed you useless. Tiffany had broken things off with him the same day doctors told Dale that he'd never play in the NFL. She didn't even wait for a second opinion.

Dale hadn't even tried to explore a serious relationship since then. He was fine with the occasional hook-up.

Until now.

He wasn't interested in just hooking up with Nyree. There was more to what they had going on. And despite his attempts to fight it, there was something going on between them.

The past week he'd spent way too many hours—hours when he should have been sleeping—texting Nyree while she covered for yet another of her coworkers on the nightshift at the lab. Back when they first started renovating Whitmer House, she would be in one part of the house while he was in another. But not anymore. When feasible, she brought whatever project she was working on to whatever room Dale happened to be working in.

They spent every second talking about some of the inanest topics, but he loved it. Just the day before they went back and forth, debating everything from who shouldn't have been killed off on *The Walking Dead* to which of Maplesville's only two sushi restaurants served the best California roll. Even when he secretly agreed with her, Dale claimed the opposite, just to get a rise out of her.

It had been so long since he'd felt that type of connection with a woman. He wasn't sure if he'd ever clicked with someone as quickly as he and Nyree had. Sure, there was a thick layer of lust covering everything they said, but it went beyond simply lusting after her body. When it came to Nyree, he wanted more.

His phone chimed with an incoming text. A smile drew across his face when he read it.

Leaving work. Heading to the park. See you there.

Just seeing those words made him happier than he'd felt in ages. And to think he'd actually considered cancelling with a lie that he was sick?

"Sick, my ass," Dale muttered, starting up the truck.

For the first time in a long time he was experiencing joy again. He knew it wouldn't last forever. It *couldn't* last forever. Nyree could do a lot better than him. Once she realized that, the little thing they had going would end.

But he would enjoy her while he could.

As the crowd continued to fill the small amphitheater at the park behind the old Slidell train station, Nyree stood on the outskirts, waiting for Dale's text. He said he'd let her know when he'd arrived. There was still a small part of her that wondered if he would stand her up. Despite all the time they'd spent getting to know each other over the past month—working side by side on the renovation and sharing hundreds of text messages when they weren't together at Whitmer House—he was still hesitant about taking things any further.

It frustrated the hell out of her.

When she'd asked him to come to the concert, Nyree had fully expected him to turn her down. His love of good music apparently superseded his ridiculous vow not to get involved with her.

Yet, that's exactly what had been happening, even if Dale refused to admit it. There was such an ease between them. Their conversations meandered from one topic to the next without ever feeling forced or awkward. How could he not see what was happening?

"Because he's stubborn," Nyree muttered.

He was totally stubborn, but he made stubborn look sexy. She smiled, thinking about the improvised version of *Name That Tune* they'd played a couple of days ago while munching on the cold pasta salad she'd brought over to the Whitmer House. After discovering how much their music tastes meshed, Nyree challenged him to test his skill against hers. Using the shuffle feature on iTunes, they went through half her playlist, testing which of them could figure out the song first. Having Dale admit that she was better at it than he was ranked up there with winning her high school Quiz Bowl tournament back in her junior year.

"What are you smiling about?"

Nyree yelped, clutching her chest. She playfully slapped Dale on the arm. "Don't sneak up on me like that," she said.

"I didn't sneak up on you." He gestured to her phone. "Didn't you get my text?"

She hadn't even checked. She'd been too busy thinking about how much fun she'd been having with him over these past few weeks.

She took him by the hand. "The concert is about to start. Let's go before all the good spots are taken."

There was no opening act. Simone Thibodaux didn't need one. The artist could hold her own on any stage, and the local crowd loved seeing their hometown girl making good. The promoters—who had obviously underestimated Simone's fans' willingness to come out on a Thursday night—moved back the barricades, opening up more space in the park.

With the added breathing room, Nyree took advantage, dancing to Simone's newest release, an up-tempo dance track. It was a departure for the singer, who came from jazz roots. Her mother, Maddie Thibodaux, was New Orleans jazz royalty. Nyree could appreciate a mellow saxophone-accompanied ballad, but she thought Simone's voice fit much better in the R&B genre.

She turned to Dale, holding her hand out for him to join her.

He shook his head.

"Don't be a coward," she said.

"I don't dance."

She grabbed his hand. "You do tonight."

For all his scowling, he didn't put up much resistance when she tugged him to her. She entwined their fingers and swung their arms to the beat.

"See, this isn't so hard, is it?" She winked, then turned to the stage, placing her back against Dale's chest. She moved her hips to the music, her backside slightly brushing against the front of his jeans.

He leaned forward and pressed his lips to her ear. "I know what you're doing."

Nyree peered over her shoulder. "I'm not trying to hide it."

To put an exclamation point on her statement, she rubbed against him again, releasing a throaty chuckle at his painful groan.

She didn't feel an ounce of guilt at getting him worked up in the middle of a crowded concert. It's exactly what he deserved for denying that there could be anything more between them. She was tired of talking; she would *show* him.

It was as if fate was urging her in that

direction as, a few minutes later, Simone Thibodaux switched from the up-tempo dance songs to slower ballads. As the soulful vocalist sang about newfound love, Nyree reached back and captured Dale's arms, bringing them around and clasping his hands over her stomach. He squeezed her ever so slightly, causing a million heated tingles to travel along her skin.

He rested his chin on her shoulder and whispered, "You feel so good against me," in her ear.

Nyree looked back at him. "So why aren't you holding me tighter?"

He obliged, tucking her even more snuggly against him. There was no denying the bulge pressing into her spine. Her body shuddered with the sensations his arousal summoned within her. Nyree felt as if she would burst clear out of her skin as she waited for his lips to touch her skin. They were so close, mere centimeters from her neck. She just knew a kiss was imminent.

But it never came.

Much to her chagrin, when the song ended, Dale loosened his hold and stepped back several inches. It took everything she had within her not to scream in frustration.

The concert ended just before nine, but Nyree wasn't ready to leave. She took Dale's hand and threaded their fingers together. They started along one of the walking paths that snaked throughout the park. The moon's soft rays shone through branches of century old oak trees, casting shadows upon everything they touched.

"Aren't you tired?" he asked. "You've been at work all day."

"So have you, but you look as if you can go for a few more hours."

He chuckled. "I don't know about that. I did make some pretty good progress on the house today."

Nyree shook her head. "I don't want to talk about the house right now." She'd talked to Reesa earlier today and learned that her friend's landlord had found a new tenant. The added pressure of realizing that Reesa wouldn't be able to return to her shop if the house wasn't ready in time had been the source of mind-numbing anxiety today. "Pick another topic."

"Such as?"

"Such as…" She thought for a moment, trying to come up with something they hadn't talked about yet. "Such as why you're still single," she said. The question had been swirling in her mind as she'd gotten to know him better over these past weeks. She couldn't fathom how a man who was such a catch hadn't been caught yet.

Not that she was complaining or anything. Still, there had to be a reason.

"So?" Nyree nudged him with her shoulder. "Why no girlfriend?"

He shrugged. "I guess I just haven't found

the right person." He tipped his head to the side. "To be honest, I haven't really looked that hard since I broke up with my last girlfriend."

It should come as no surprise that he had an ex, yet just hearing him refer to her caused a funky feeling to settle in Nyree's stomach. "How long ago did you two break up?"

Dale looked over at her and grinned. "You're just full of questions tonight, aren't you?"

"Yes, and I'm holding you hostage here until you answer them."

He peered out at the pond that was bordered by the walking path they'd taken. Delicate white petals from the star magnolia trees edging the pathway flittered across the still waters.

"Pretty nice place to be held prisoner."

"It's gorgeous here," Nyree agreed. "Now stop stalling. When did you and your girlfriend breakup?"

Dale sighed and stuffed the hand that wasn't holding hers into his front pocket. "Senior year of college," he answered.

Nyree's mouth fell open. "That was, what, like five years ago?"

He shrugged. "Yeah, I guess."

"You haven't dated in five years?"

"I've dated," he said. "Or, I don't know. I guess you'd call it dating."

"Ah." She nodded. "You've spent the past five years hooking up with girls. That's what you're trying to say, right?" She laughed. "You're more like my brothers than you realize."

Dale stopped walking and let go of her hand.

She turned to him. "What?"

"Keep up that kind of talk and I'm going home."

Nyree burst out laughing. "Sorry. I didn't mean anything by it."

He gave her a look that clearly said *Yeah, right*, but didn't comment further.

"So why haven't you had a serious relationship in five years? Is it because you were so heartbroken over your last girlfriend?"

His sharp laugh broke through the stillness surrounding them.

"That was a legitimate question," Nyree said, "But, by your reaction, I think I have my answer."

"You want the truth?" Dale asked.

"Nine times out of ten, yes, I prefer the truth."

"Okay, so when would you rather I not tell you the truth?" he asked, amusement shimmering in his eyes.

"When it's just too depressing. In those instances, you have my permission to lie to me to protect my sanity."

He nodded, again with the smile. "Good to know." Then he shrugged. "There was nothing too devastating about my break up with Tiffany," he continued. "After my injury—when it was obvious I wouldn't play ball again—she got the hell out of dodge. Guess she thought plain old Dale Chauvin wasn't good enough for her." He paused for a moment. The sudden intensity in his gaze caught her off-guard. "A lot of people would agree with her," he finally said.

"A lot of people are assholes," Nyree said. "Including your ex-girlfriend."

"Is she? She was a political science major, and had just been accepted into one of the top law schools in the country. What did I have to offer someone with so much going for them?"

"Uh, let's see," Nyree said, ticking the items off on her fingers. "You're hard-working, kind, funny, and sexy as the day is long. Need I go on?"

He shook his head. "Nah, you've given my ego more than enough stroking."

"You're welcome," she answered with a smug grin.

Nyree took his hand again, but when she attempted to continue their stroll, he remained standing there, the light from the moon casting a gentle shadow across his strong jaw.

Dale looked down at their clasped hands then brought his gaze up to her face. "This has been nice," he said.

"Our date, you mean?"

"Yeah, I guess that's what this is, huh?"

"Yes," she answered. The first of many, if she had anything to say about it. "And now that we've established that this *is* our first official date, does this mean you're done playing hard to get?"

"That's not what I've been doing," Dale immediately objected, then he grimaced. "Okay, so maybe I have, but you know I had valid reasons before."

"And now?"

"Now, I just—" He shook his head and looked out over the water, releasing an uneasy laugh. When his gaze returned to her, it held an earnestness that touched her heart. "This is getting too hard to fight."

Nyree's chest tightened with an agonizing amount of hope.

"You're the one who chooses to fight it," she reminded him in a gentle whisper. "It's my job to make it harder for you, not easier."

"Do you have to be so damn good at your job? Oh, wait, I forgot I'm talking to the ultimate overachiever here."

"Damn right," she said.

"Does this mean I have to stand here while you rub it in?" he asked. Her forehead furrowed with her confused frown. "You said that you would rub it in when I finally caved," he reminded her.

"Oh, that's right," Nyree said. She hunched her shoulders. "I guess listening to Simone's singing has put me in a generous mood. I've decided to take it easy on you." She smiled up at him. "Lucky you."

His brown eyes traveled over her face. "In

more ways than one."

His softly spoken words sent a river of warmth cascading through her bloodstream. She tucked herself against his side, needing to be close to him as they continued their walk around the park.

Nyree noticed that they weren't the only concert goers who'd decided to stick around. They passed several couples walking hand-in-hand along the walking path. A few others sat on the wooden park benches that dotted the grounds. When she and Dale reached the copse of sturdy shade trees toward the far end of the park, Nyree stepped up onto the gnarled roots of an oak tree that had pushed its way out of the ground. It gave her just enough height to put her at face level with him.

"You sure you don't need to get home and get some sleep?" Dale asked.

Nyree rolled her eyes. "You sound frustratingly like the two people you don't want me to compare you to."

His eyes narrowed.

She put both hands up. "You have to admit you have a few of their tendencies."

The vehemence in which he shook his head made her laugh.

"No way," Dale said. "Take that back."

"But it's true," she barely managed to say past her giggles. "Maybe it's just something with former football players. Like a personality trait or something."

"You'd better be grateful my dad taught me better than to leave a woman by herself late at night. Otherwise, I'd be out."

"All because I said you're like Desmond and Lance?" She laughed even harder. "Maybe I'm the one who should be insulted here. They are my brothers after all. They do have *some* redeeming qualities."

"Name one," Dale said, his lips tipping up in a grin.

Nyree tilted her head to the side, pretending to think. "Um, Desmond is a really good carpenter."

"That's the best you can do?"

"At the moment," she said. "If I weren't still so mad at him for backing out of doing the renovations, I could probably come up with a few more."

"So why didn't you just wait until Desmond and Lance could get to it? Is it really that important to hold the grand opening on your aunt's birthday?"

"It is to me," she said. "After all, it was money I inherited from my aunt that provided the down payment on the house."

"Really?" he asked.

Nyree looked up at him. "What? You think Lakeshore Refinery pays me that much money?"

Dale shrugged. "Not sure what the going rate is for a cute chemist."

She smiled. "I do okay, but Any Way You Want It Salon and Spa will become a reality because of my aunt's penchant for saving."

"Now I see why that date is so important. I guess opening on her birthday really is the best tribute you can give her."

Not only that, but now that Reesa had given up the lease on her shop, it was even more crucial that they open on time.

Nyree didn't want to think about the house, or her brothers, or anything else that was likely to give her a panic attack.

She put a finger over his lips, silencing him. "No talk about work, remember?" she said. "I just need a break from everything tonight."

She was struck by how extremely soft his lips were. The need to finally feel them against her own became a living, breathing thing.

Dale's intense stare grew hot as his eyes focused on her. He captured the finger she held to his lips and moved it away from his mouth, but he didn't release it. Instead, he brought her hand to his chest as he stepped in close to her.

His voice dropping to a near whisper, he said, "You don't want to talk about work. What else is there for us to do?"

"I can think of one thing," she said as she leaned into him, searching his face for permission. She half-expected him to pull away. Instead, he pushed his fingers into her hair and brushed his lips against hers.

She'd never expected anything so gentle and sweet from a guy so big and brawny. But that's exactly what she got from Dale's kiss. Gentle, sweet, and everything she needed.

He took his time with her, pressing lightly at first, as if learning the feel and shape of her lips was the most important thing in his world right now. But it wasn't long before he wrapped his arms around her and stepped in closer, fitting his big body more firmly against her. The thick bulge behind his zipper brushed against her hip. Its effect was startling, as if someone lit a fuse to her nerve endings.

Liquid fire raced through Nyree's blood as her hands sought to find purchase, grabbing onto Dale's sturdy shoulders to steady herself. The contour of those well-defined muscles underneath her fingers made her itch to touch his bare skin.

She moaned as his tongue finally made an appearance, pushing past her lips and exploring her mouth, as if seeking something he hadn't experienced in a long time. He teased her with his tongue, dipping it in and out between her lips, causing tremors of want to race along her skin.

He moved his mouth down the column of her throat, then back up along her jaw, grazing her earlobe as he whispered against her skin, "Forget what I said before. This isn't just hard to fight. It's *impossible*."

Nyree's mouth curled up in a smile. "Mmm," she murmured. "Nothing like the sweet taste of victory."

He released a hoarse laugh, then looked her

in the eyes. "I'm still not sure this is the best idea," he said "In fact, I think this is a pretty bad idea."

She reached down and cupped him through his jeans. "No, you don't. Or at least one part of you doesn't."

Dale pitched his head back and groaned, even as his hips thrust against her hand. "Just remember, if I die of lust, you won't have anyone to work on the house."

Nyree dropped her hand.

"Fine," she said. "But don't expect me to wait until the house is done. You seem capable of handling both me and the renovations at the same time."

"You willing to take that chance?" he asked.

At that moment she was willing to do just about anything to have him kiss her again. Nyree wrapped her fingers around the back of his neck and gently urged him to lower his head.

"For more of this? I think I am," she whispered before taking his lips in another searing kiss.

Chapter Six

Dale kneaded the bridge of his nose as he scrolled through another article on writing an effective business plan on his iPad. It was the fifth one he'd read and he still didn't know exactly where he should start with all of this.

Maybe it's a sign that you shouldn't start at all.

He cursed that damn voice in his head, but couldn't deny that the question continued to nag him.

He'd hardly thought about starting up his own business lately. Instead, he'd spent most of his time working on mock plays and conditioning drills to run with Kendrick, and when he wasn't doing that he was working on Whitmer House or texting with Nyree like a love-struck teenager.

If this general contractor business was his dream, wouldn't it be on his mind all the time?

But it really wasn't his dream. He could at least acknowledge that. Starting up his own general contractor business was never about fulfilling a dream. It was about making a living the best way he could under the circumstances he'd created for his own life.

Back when he first started working

construction—after he'd fully healed from his knee surgeries—he'd told his friends and family that he'd chosen to do so because his body craved the physical labor. He'd used the excuse of wanting to stay in shape as his reasoning for not putting his worthless college degree to use. Whenever Vanessa or his parents brought up his business degree, Dale had an excuse for why he wasn't ready to leave construction work.

But in thirty years, did he really want to be in the same place? Even if he was no longer the one pounding the nails, even if he was the guy behind the desk calling the shots, is that *really* what he wanted to do with his life?

Dale drew in a frustrated breath before releasing it with a sigh.

He wasn't new to this game. He'd played it off and on over the years, mentally debating the choices he'd made. Usually, he was able to shove his thoughts of wanting more out of life aside, but ever since he'd started working for Nyree, he couldn't quench his thirst to do more. To *be* more.

He wasn't good enough for her. But he *could* be.

Witnessing how she commanded her life—working in a field she loved and starting her own business at such a young age—had been the kind of wake-up call that had Dale questioning just what the hell he was doing.

And what he *wasn't* doing.

He didn't think he even had dreams

anymore—especially any centered around football, but working with Kendrick these past few months had revived his love of the game. When he thought about the kind of impact he could have on kids like Kendrick—young men who only saw the glamorous side of the game, and didn't realize the pitfalls lurking just around the corner—it made thoughts of becoming a coach so enticing his skin itched with it. He wouldn't allow the kids he coached to fall into those same traps that had snared him.

But he wasn't a coach, was he?

But what if you could be?

Dale could usually pull himself back when he started to fall into this fantasy, but it wasn't as easy for him to let it go after all the thoughts that had been swirling around in his head all morning. This time he couldn't help but indulge, if only for a moment.

He set his elbows on his thighs and cradled his head in his palms, and just allowed himself to imagine it. Going back to school, getting his degree—one he actually *earned* this time. Maybe even coaching at his old high school? Look what he'd been able to do with Kendrick in a short amount of time. He could totally do this. It was possible.

"Dammit, no it's not." He slapped his palms down on his thighs.

He blamed Ian and Sam for putting this shit in his head. He couldn't go back to school. How would people react to him going back to get a college degree he'd supposedly already earned?

Except that he couldn't teach with the degree he held now, even if he *had* rightfully earned it. He'd have to earn a teaching degree.

He wouldn't have to admit to his parents, his sister, or his two best friends that his degree wasn't worth the paper it was written on. That he'd skipped class more than he'd attended, because he had professors willing to give him a passing grade in the name of helping out the football program. That he'd allowed himself to be used like some stupid jock who didn't care about his own future.

He wouldn't have to admit to any of it.

But did he really have it in him to go back to school and earn his teaching degree? What if, once he started, he realized he didn't have what it takes?

The thought of that happening made sweat break out across Dale's chest.

He needed to stick with what he knew. He was lucky that he *could* earn a living pounding a hammer, despite how much he hated the thought of doing it for the rest of his life.

It was the price he had to pay for putting himself in this situation in the first place. If he'd done what he was supposed to do while in school, he would not be looking at years of doing something he no longer enjoyed.

"God," Dale said with an exhausted sigh. "I don't want to think about this right now."

Maybe this is why he'd stuck with

construction for so long, because he hated thinking about his future. But Dale had to admit it was a helluva lot better than contemplating his *right now*. Because his *right now* had him going out of his damn mind with lust.

His vow to keep things with Nyree purely professional had gone down in a blaze of glory after those kisses they'd shared the night before.

Those kisses. *God, those kisses.*

Dale groaned, setting the iPad next to him on the sofa and stretching his legs out in an attempt to free up some room in his jeans. He tugged on the fabric, shifting the zipper to the side to release the pressure.

If wishes were being handed out at the concert last night, that second kiss with Nyree would have gone three thousand times further than it had. From the moment his lips touched hers, his mind began to race with expectations. All he could think about was all that could come later, if only he said the word. Because Dale knew that's all it would take. Nyree had made her feelings known. She was fully onboard. He just had to join her.

The night before, he almost had.

Actually, in a way, he *had*.

In reality their kiss ended in that park in Slidell, but in his mind he and Nyree made it back to his bed, where he'd kept her for hours. Once he actually did fall into bed last night, Dale had carried the fantasy with him, bringing himself to release over and over again, all through the night. He hadn't jerked off this much since high school.

He'd tried fighting it, but he was done with that. He didn't give a damn about being professional anymore. And when it came to her brothers? Like Nyree said before, it was an extra bonus to piss off Desmond and Lance Grant.

It no longer mattered that she would eventually realize he wasn't good enough for her. He'd deal with that when the time came.

At that moment, the only thing that mattered was this all-consuming need he had for her. It was a need that went far beyond the fantasies he'd indulged in last night. He needed more than just her body. He craved her determined spirit and that amazing smile and all the attitude she doled out when the need arose.

He yearned to know her on so many levels; so much more than he'd wanted to get to know any other woman he'd been with in the past. There was something about Nyree that affected him in a way he'd never experienced before.

Dale picked up his phone, itching to call her. But they'd been out late after the concert. He wouldn't mess with her sleep, especially with the shifts she'd been working in the lab at the refinery. Despite putting in for vacation time, she'd been called in to cover for sick coworkers several times over the past few weeks.

Instead of bothering her, Dale pushed himself up from the sofa and went into his bedroom so he could change. There was too much work to do on the Whitmer House for him to waste another minute sitting around his place. He was still on schedule to complete the job a couple of days ahead of time, but Dale had worked in the field long enough to know that Murphy's Law loved to hang around construction sites.

They'd already faced a couple of setbacks he hadn't anticipated, like the jerry-rigged wiring he'd discovered when he started work on upping the electrical amps the house needed to run the salon's hair dryers. Thankfully, the copper wiring was in good shape, but rerouting the connectors and adding a second circuit breaker stole an entire day from his schedule. He'd had to stay two extra hours per day for the past week trying to make up the time.

Yeah, the sooner he finished up this renovation, the better.

Dale's fingers stilled on the zipper of the well-worn work jeans he'd just pulled on.

What would happen once he was done with the job? Would that be the end of things…whatever it was that he'd finally allowed to start between him and Nyree with the kisses they shared in the park? Had he wasted all this time fighting it, only to see it end in another month?

"Stop overthinking everything," Dale whispered to himself.

He would just enjoy it, no matter how long it lasted.

He didn't bother changing the old T-shirt he'd thrown on after his morning run. He pulled on the chain with the St. Thomas the Apostle medallion—a gift from his devout Catholic grandmother who demanded Dale wear the patron saint of construction workers—then sat on the edge of the bed and tugged on his steel-toe work boots. Like his jeans, they were well worn, too. Maybe it was time to get a new pair.

Maybe you won't have to?

Dale mentally batted the thought away. He wasn't going down that rabbit hole again. He pushed up from the edge of the bed.

Enough of this shoulda, woulda, coulda nonsense. He had a job to do.

When he turned into the driveway at Whitmer House, he did a double take at the sight of Nyree's SUV parked next to the side porch. He'd expected her to be sleeping in after working all day the day before and not getting home until past midnight. He'd followed her home after the concert, and with the most amazing reserve of willpower he'd ever summoned, managed to stop himself from following her inside.

If she were to ask him inside today, he wouldn't turn her down.

Soon, he wouldn't have to worry about being invited into her apartment. She was probably moving more of her belongings into the upstairs rooms where she would soon be living. That's the only reason Dale could imagine why she'd be here already today.

She'd completed all the tasks she could do on the house for now. Once he was done constructing the new walls in the massage clinic, she would come behind him and paint them, but for the next few days all the work fell on Dale's shoulders.

As he came upon the side door, Dale's forehead furrowed into a deep vee at the sound of hammering. He went into the old family room, which would be her friend Amara's makeup studio. He found Nyree driving a nail into a baseboard.

"What are you doing?" Dale asked, walking over to where she knelt on the floor. He inspected her work, not totally surprised to find that she'd done a good job. Was there anything she couldn't do well?

She turned, her eyes wide with surprise, the hammer dangling from her hand. She set it on the floor and wiped at her brow.

With a sigh, she sat on her heels and tilted her head back, looking up at the ceiling. "Thought I could help speed things along," she said.

She held out her hand. Dale captured it and pulled her up. The urge to kiss her was so overwhelming that he wasn't sure he'd be able to fight it, but at that moment he was even more concerned with the worry lines creasing her forehead.

"You do realize we're still on schedule,

right?"

"I know, I know," she said, her shoulders slumping. "It's just that you never know what can go wrong. Take what happened with the shampoo sinks. We couldn't anticipate the company sending the wrong ones. Do you know how much of a bind I'd be in if the shipment had been delayed?"

"But the sinks got here in plenty of time for us to send them back, and the ones you ordered will be here by the end of the week. We're good, Nyree."

She nodded, but worry still clouded her eyes. "April 4th will be here before we know it."

Dale smoothed his hands up and down her arms. "I told you I'm going to make sure the house is done in time. I'll find a way to squeeze in a few more hours every day. As long as I make time for my sessions with Kendrick, I'm good."

She frowned. "Who's Kendrick?"

"He's this kid I'm, well, tutoring, I guess. Tutoring in football."

"You're a football tutor?"

"Basically," he said. "He plays the middle linebacker position for Magnolia Bend High School. Kendrick's dad hired me to give him one-on-one instruction."

"I didn't even know people do that," she said.

He snorted. "If only you knew the lengths some people go to when it comes to high school football around here."

"I grew up around it, remember?"

"Yeah, I guess you do know," Dale said. He gave her upper arms a squeeze. "Now, can you promise me that I won't come in to find you hammering baseboards?"

She pulled her bottom lip between her teeth. "I don't know about that. I don't like to make promises I'm not sure I'll be able to keep."

"Nyree," he said with a sigh.

"Okay, okay," she said. "I'll try to stay in my lane when it comes to the rest of the renovation. It's just that my friends are coming to see the house today. I was hoping to at least have one room that looked less, well, unfinished."

"But your friends knew the house would require a lot of work before you all could move in, right?"

"Yes, but you have to understand my friends to know where I'm coming from." She pulled her cellphone from her pocket and held it up to him. "They've sent at least fifty group texts this morning debating the theme for the downstairs bathroom."

"I didn't know bathrooms had a theme."

"You and me both. Yet, they see that as the biggest dilemma." She huffed out a laugh. "I just know they're going to walk in here and freak out over the state of the house."

Dale captured her shoulders and pulled her in close. He caressed her jaw with the backs of his fingers, lingering over her smooth skin as he tipped her chin up and stared into her eyes.

"Let your friends sweat the small stuff. I want to make sure *you* understand that we're going to get the big things done in time for the grand opening. I've got this, Nyree. I won't let you down."

He dipped his head and captured her lips in a slow, easy kiss. It was *so* damn easy, as if he'd been kissing her like this all his life.

Dale angled his head to the side as he moved his hands from her arms to the small of her back. He pressed his body close to hers, reveling in the feel of her soft curves moving against him. Her mouth opened readily, inviting his tongue inside and setting his blood on fire.

Both he and Nyree jumped at the sound of several throats clearing.

Dale looked up over Nyree's head to find three women standing just outside the doorway of the makeup studio. All with their hands on their hips.

The one with the blond streaks in her shoulder-length hair, said, "Is this what you call hard at work?"

"And this is what I was trying to avoid," Nyree said

She sighed, turning around to find Reesa, Cheyenne and Amara standing in the middle of the vestibule, which had become the staging area for all of the building material. Their expressions ranged from amused, to curious, to upset.

Nyree held her hands up as they all came into the makeup studio. "Before you all start to freak out, understand that it looks worse than it is."

"I wouldn't call this 'practically finished,' Nyree," Cheyenne said.

"Is that what you told them?" Dale asked.

"Not exactly," she answered.

"Yes, exactly," Reesa said. "Just yesterday you said this place was practically finished."

"I can't bring clients in here," Amara said.

"You work out of your house right now," Nyree pointed out.

"Yes, but my house doesn't have holes in the ceilings," she pointed up to the circular cutouts that would soon house recessed lights.

"Those are for the lights you said you just had to have," Nyree said. She turned to Reesa, who still stood there with her hands on her hips, her jaw tight with tension.

"I know what you're going to say, but I'm telling you, this house will be ready in time. Just trust me on this."

"Can I?" Reesa asked. "Do you know how many appointments I already have lined up for April? Do you know how quickly those people will turn to Salon Nouveau if I'm not able to come through?"

"I know, Reesa."

"Apparently, you don't. Because if you *did*

you would be working instead of standing here in the middle of a halfway finished house getting it on with Mr. Hot Construction Guy here. "

"Actually, it's Dale," Dale said, a heavy dose of sarcasm coloring his voice.

Reesa barely glanced his way, but Cheyenne's brows lifted with interest. She took a step forward, but Nyree stopped her with a don't-even-think-about-it glare.

"Dale has been working around the clock to get the house done on time," Nyree said.

"I haven't done it alone," Dale interjected. "Nyree has been putting in her share of hours here, too. She probably could have used some help over these past few weeks."

"What about your brothers?" Amara asked. "I thought Desmond and Lance were helping?"

"My brothers didn't have time to work on the house," she said.

Cheyenne folded her arms across her chest and cocked her brow. "According to Lance, you were being stubborn and told them you didn't want them working on the house."

"When did you talk to Lance?" Nyree asked. "And why?"

Cheyenne's mouth gaped. "I—" she started, then stopped.

"Look, whatever Cheyenne has going on with your brother is unimportant," Reesa said. "The important thing is that this business is operational by the first week in April.

Remember, you're the only one with another career to keep you afloat. We don't have fallback plans." She gestured to Cheyenne and Amara. "This is the one promise you made that you *have* to come through on, Nyree."

"Don't I always come through?" Nyree asked, more than a little ticked off that her friends would start questioning her now. She'd never given them reason to doubt her.

Yet, Nyree couldn't quell the sudden unease that began to roil in her gut.

She'd always considered herself fearless, but when she first came up with this idea, the one thing that had caused her a tremor of fear was knowing that her three friends' livelihoods would rest in her hands. She didn't want to be responsible for them losing clients.

And she wouldn't. She would do whatever she had to do to make sure that didn't happen.

"I'm handling it," Nyree said again. "I promise, it will all be done in time. And you know I never go back on a promise."

The three of them didn't look convinced, but they didn't refute her claim, either. Because they couldn't. She got things done. She *always* got things done.

"We're good?" Nyree asked.

"I'm still not sure," Reesa said. "But I'm going to trust you anyway. You've earned that much. Now, how about a tour so we can see how much progress *has* been made?"

"Absolutely," Nyree said, straightening her

shoulders and feeling back in control. "The biggest project is nearly done. Dale's divided the two upstairs bedrooms into a sitting area and three smaller private massage rooms for Cheyenne's massage clinic."

"I have to see this," Cheyenne said, leading the way up the stairs.

Before Nyree could join them, Dale stopped her, pulling at the back hem of her T-shirt as she started ascending the steps. Nyree turned, finding herself at eye level with him.

"I thought commemorating your aunt's birthday was the only reason you needed the house done by the first week in April." Dale asked. "Why didn't you give me the full story on the timetable?"

"Because I didn't realize it would turn into such a big issue. Who could have expected the problems we've run into?"

"I could have," he said. "There are always setbacks, especially when dealing with an older house."

She closed her eyes, hating the tiny drop of defeat that managed to sink into her bones. It felt so foreign to her to even think this way. She had never taken on anything of this magnitude and the thought of failing scared her breathless.

She lowered her voice when she asked, "Realistically, can this be done by the fourth?"

"I promised you I'd have the house done, and I will." Dale inhaled a deep breath and blew it out. "But I have to be honest, Nyree, it won't be easy, especially with me doing the rest of the work alone."

"That's why I was here helping today."

"You're a chemist, not a construction worker," Dale reminded her. "You've done a kickass job painting all the trim work, but there are things you just physically aren't capable of doing."

"Didn't you say you have friends you could hire?"

"That was before the flu that's been going around made it to the latest Harding construction site," Dale said. "Half the guys are out with it, and none of those who are able to work will give up the time and a half overtime pay they can make with Harding."

He put his hands on his hips and dropped his head. A muscle in his jaw ticked.

"What about Desmond and Lance?" Dale asked.

She shook her head. "No. I'm not going to go back to them and beg. That's exactly what Desmond said I would have to do and I refuse to give him the satisfaction."

"Would you rather ruin your friends' businesses?" Dale asked.

Oh, that was a low blow. Accurate, but low.

"Look," Dale said. "I don't necessarily want to work alongside your brothers, but I've seen their work. They're good. And they're willing to do the labor free-of-charge."

"With conditions, and I don't like the

conditions."

He folded his arms over his chest. "You really are stubborn, aren't you?"

Nyree closed her eyes. "Yes, I am," she admitted. "But with good reason."

She knew she owed him more of an explanation, but God, she didn't want to get into the complicated issues she had with her brothers. How could she explain her resentment over all the attention Desmond and Lance got because they were football stars who could do no wrong, when Dale was once an even bigger star?

How could she describe what it was like growing up in their shadow, having to follow Desmond's rules because he was the oldest and their mother automatically deferred to him after their father left? It left her both wanting to prove her worth to them, and not giving a damn about anything Desmond and Lance said regarding her life.

"Is there any way possible that we can get this done without having to bring my brothers onboard?" Nyree asked.

Dale hunched his shoulders. "We can try, but—"

He stopped at the sound of Reesa, Amara and Cheyenne coming down the stairs.

"So? What do—" Nyree paused, tilting her head toward the wall where she thought she heard rumbling. She figured it must have been a truck passing the house. "What do you all think?" she finished.

"It looks awesome," Cheyenne exclaimed. "Those prints I bought from that street artist in the French Quarter will look spectacular on the walls. I am so happy you convinced us to do this, Nyree."

"I am, too," Reesa said, "But I'm still not convinced all of this will be ready in time." She gestured at the spools of insulated wires, baseboards and sheets of lumber scattered around the vestibule.

"It will be," Nyree said. "There's nothing to worry about. Just trust me."

Just as the words left her mouth, a loud creak rang out and the wall inside the downstairs bathroom burst open. Water blasted through the open bathroom door, dousing them all.

"Oh, my God," Nyree yelled.

"Shit!" Dale barked, taking off for the kitchen.

Reesa, Cheyenne and Amara all stood there screaming while Nyree ran into the bathroom, futilely trying to stop the water from coming out of the busted pipe. Several seconds later, it stopped.

Nyree stood in the middle of the bathroom, her t-shirt and jeans completely soaked.

"Are you okay?" She turned at Dale's inquiry. He gestured toward the kitchen with his head. "For future reference, the main water line is just outside the back door that leads to the kitchen."

Of course it made more sense to cut off the main water line instead of trying to stop a raging stream with her bare hands. She considered herself pretty kickass, but she wasn't *that* kickass.

Nyree held her arms out, looking down at her clothes again.

"I'm soaked," she said.

When Dale didn't comment, she looked up to find him staring at her chest with the most heated look anyone had ever directed her way. Nyree realized how she must appear to him, standing there in a soaking wet pink t-shirt, her bra visible through the transparent material. It turned her on despite the fact that her three best friends were in the next room.

"We should, uh, get this cleaned up," she said.

Dale nodded. His Adam's apple bobbed as he swallowed and then cleared his throat. "Yeah," he said. But he didn't make a move. Neither did she. They just continued to stare at each other. Nyree's nipples tightened with each second that passed, straining against the sodden bra and t-shirt.

"Well, don't just stand there! Move!"

Dale and Nyree both jumped at Cheyenne's demand. Her friend pushed her way into the crowded space, ushering both Nyree and Dale out of the bathroom.

"Is there anything around here that we can

use to clean this up?" Reesa asked.

Dale's head jerked slightly, as if being knocked out of a daze. "I, uh, I've got some rags in my truck," he murmured. He looked over at Nyree again. "You should take those wet clothes off before you get sick."

It was on the tip of her tongue to ask him if he wanted to help, but after the way her friends had caught the two of them kissing earlier, Nyree knew it best she refrain.

Besides, with this latest setback, having Dale rip her clothes off should be the furthest thing from her mind.

Nyree went upstairs and dried off as best she could, changing into a set of scrubs she'd packed in one of the boxes she'd brought from her apartment. Unfortunately, she hadn't put any clean underwear in there.

By the time she got back downstairs, Reesa, Cheyenne, Amara and Dale were moving with military precision, clearing out the water from the busted pipe. Nyree looked at the hole the high-pressured water had blown out of the plaster wall, and nearly sank to the floor.

She never gave into defeat. Never.

But there was only so much a girl could take before she reached her breaking point. After yet another mishap that was certain to cost both time and money she couldn't afford, Nyree was pretty sure she was there.

Chapter Seven

Dale tapped his thumbs in a nervous rhythm on the steering wheel as he stared across the parking lot at Nyree's SUV. He opened the door then immediately closed it. On a previous try he'd gotten as far as the fifth step up to her second floor apartment before turning around and coming back to sit in his truck like a damn stalker in a *Dateline* special.

"This is ridiculous."

He threw open the door and stepped out of the truck. His purposeful strides ate up the asphalt as he propelled himself across the parking lot. He marched up the stairs, put his hand up to knock on her front door, then dropped it and backed away. Turning, he started for the stairs, but stopped mid-step at the sound of the front door opening.

"Dale?"

Nyree's voice sent a shiver down his spine. He turned back around to find her standing in the open doorway holding a wooden cooking spoon and dressed in cutoff jean shorts and a cropped t-shirt. The sight of her lusciously bare thighs and midriff nearly brought him to his knees.

"How…uh, how did you know I was here?" Dale asked. "I never knocked."

She pointed the spoon to a small rectangular box with a tiny blinking red light just above the door.

"Motion sensor," she said. "It alerts me whenever someone comes within two feet of the front door. A gift from Desmond, who hates the fact that I live alone in big, bad St. Pierre," she said with a heavy dose of sarcasm.

A small smile curved up the corner of his mouth at her obvious distaste. "You did say your brothers were overprotective." His eyes trailed up and down her body again. "I'm not so sure that's a bad thing."

All that time he'd spent sitting in the parking lot was worth seeing the instant blush that reddened her brown cheeks.

She tilted her head to the side. "So, what are you doing here?" she asked.

Making a mistake, he thought.

He'd known it was a mistake the minute he started heading east on Highway 421, but not once did Dale consider turning his truck around. Not after the way she'd stared at him standing in that bathroom, arousal pulsing between them. Not after seeing the way her nipples had grown tight under his gaze.

It wasn't a guarantee that anything would happen between them. For all he knew, he could be in his truck in ten minutes, on his way back to Maplesville to take the longest cold shower of his life. But he *needed* to see her again. Even if only for a moment.

"I just thought I'd check on you," Dale said. "You know, after the busted pipe thing."

If there was a Big Book of Lame Excuses, that would have been the lamest excuse in it. He should have known she'd ask the question. Why in the hell hadn't he thought of an answer during the half hour he'd spent sitting in her parking lot?

Nyree's grin broadened. "Maybe if I was the Wicked Witch of the West I'd have something to worry about, but a little water has never hurt me." She stepped to the side. "Do you want to come in?"

More than he wanted to see the sun rise tomorrow morning.

"Um, sure," Dale said. He stuffed his hands in his front pockets and entered the apartment.

Cardboard moving boxes filled the majority of the space. They were stacked against the walls and on the sofa table.

"I'm glad you came over," she said, and Dale's heart immediately started to gallop like a Triple Crown winner's. "I'm making my first batch of moisturizer for men. I'd planned to bring you a jar tomorrow in hopes that you'd be willing to play guinea pig."

He followed her into the kitchen where tubs of creams and bottles of oils and gels cluttered the counter.

Nyree scooped a heap of grayish cream from

a mixing bowl and plopped it into a small glass bowl. "Try this. It has quince seed oil, witch hazel and just a touch of aloe. You can use it as a daily moisturizer or aftershave."

"So, what are you saying? That my regular drug store lotion isn't cutting it?" Dale teased.

She stuck two fingers in the cream and brought them to his cheek. "Your drug store lotion doesn't feel this good."

Desire squeezed his chest in a vice grip. His skin burned where she touched him. "No, it doesn't," Dale said.

Nyree licked her bottom lip, leaving a glistening trail of moisture that he would give anything to suck off that delectable mouth of hers. He leaned forward without even thinking about what he was doing.

And then his stomach growled. Loud.

As in loud enough for her entire apartment complex to hear.

"Damn. Excuse me," Dale said. *Shit.* He should just go home before he made a fool of himself. "I haven't eaten since lunch."

"Neither have I," Nyree said, taking a step back. "The quince oil was waiting for me when I got home. I was too excited about trying out my moisturizer formula to even think about food." She opened a drawer, pulled out a menu, and shut the drawer closed with her hip. "You like Chinese?"

A half-hour later, Dale sat on her sofa, which was actually more of a loveseat, eating his second plate of pan-fried noodles. Nyree sat next to him, with her legs folded underneath her, sipping red wine from a glass she'd taken from one of the boxes.

Dale reached for the paper to-go container filled with steamed vegetables. "Are you sure you're done with this?" he asked.

"I'm full," she said.

"How? You hardly ate anything."

"I had a full plate," she protested. "Just because it wasn't piled as high as Mount Everest like yours doesn't mean I didn't eat hardly anything." A teasing smile drew across her lips. "You know, I could make a comparison between you and my brothers, but I'd hate to ruin your dinner."

"Let me guess, they eat like a couple of former football players."

"Who now work construction," Nyree said.

Dale put his plate down. "Shit, I am more like Desmond and Lance than I thought."

"That's okay," she said with a laugh. "I told you, they've both mellowed out a lot. They're a couple of pains in the butt sometimes, but they're not all bad."

"I'm still not convinced," he said.

Once he'd scarfed down the remaining food, he stacked the empty boxes onto his empty plate and stood, but grimaced when he heard his knee crack.

"Tell me, do Desmond and Lance have old football injuries that make them feel twice as old as they actually are?"

"Your knee bothering you?" she asked, her voice tinted with concern.

"My knee, my back, my shoulders. I can't blame it all on football, though. Working construction takes a toll."

Without another word, she set her wineglass on the cardboard box next to the sofa and went over to a corner of the living room. She slid a slim rectangular carrying case from behind a fake ficus tree and unzipped it, revealing a folded table.

"You just gave me the perfect excuse to test out another product I've been working on," Nyree said. "My new line of massage oils." She popped the table open, hooked a headrest onto it, and slapped on the dark blue cushion covering the table. "Climb aboard. I'm about to make you feel better than you've ever felt in your life."

"How does that feel?" Nyree whispered against his ear.

Dale moaned, unable to come up with adequate words to describe how amazing it felt to have her hands working their magic on him. From the moment she'd touched his sore muscles he'd been catapulted into another realm, his own brand of heaven on earth.

Up until now, his only massage experiences

consisted of football trainers grinding the heel of their hands into his flesh. Just having his body prone on a cushioned massage table in Nyree's living room, with lavender and sage candles burning, and soft music playing from her iPhone was enough for him. Add in her oil-slick fingers kneading his stiff back and shoulder muscles?

Heaven. On. Earth.

"I know what you're trying to do, you know?" Dale said.

"Oh, yeah? What's that?"

"You're trying to lull me into a state of relaxation so that I'll let my guard down and you can take advantage of me."

Her deep chuckle reverberated along his skin. "And if I am?"

"I don't care," Dale murmured. "As long as you don't stop."

Another laugh. "I won't," she said. "And I promise this isn't a nefarious plan to get into your pants. This is purely medicinal. It's the least I can do after your quick action this afternoon with the busted pipe."

Dale didn't want to kill the vibe, but they would eventually have to discuss what had happened earlier and what the busted pipe meant for her timeline. The odds of him completing the work on the house by the fourth of April had just taken a nosedive. Even if Nyree could afford to spend more, he didn't see how he could finish the renovations in time for the grand opening.

And now that he knew that opening date had to do with more than just commemorating her aunt's birthday—but could very well cost her friends a ton in lost business—the pressure to get it done in time was even stronger.

But Dale didn't want to think about any of that. He just wanted to enjoy the moment. He folded his arms on the table and rested his cheek on his hands as she concentrated on his lower back, her thumbs pressing into his flesh.

"So, how does a chemist who makes her own beauty products find the time to learn how to be a masseuse too?" Dale asked.

"She begs her friend to teach her," Nyree answered. She fanned her fingers out along his sides, moving from his lower back to his hips. "Cheyenne is the only licensed masseuse out of the four of us, but we all took the time to learn what the others do. If you had a set of clippers, I could trim up your hair, too."

Dale shook his head in astonishment. "You paint trim work like a pro, install insulation better than some of the guys I work with at Harding, give a killer massage and cut hair, too? I'm going to start calling you the Renaissance Woman," he said. "There's nothing you can't do."

She huffed a humorless laugh. "Unfortunately, I can't do plumbing," she said.

The dejection in her voice gutted him, but there was nothing he could say to ease her worry. Hell, at this point, *he* was worried. He just couldn't see them getting all the work done in time with this additional setback.

But that wasn't the only thing that had Dale worried. Being reminded of just how badass she was—how she was the ultimate over-achiever while the only thing he succeeded in was not living up to his potential—reminded him that Nyree was way out of his league.

It also made him wonder once again just why, with all she had going for her, she would choose to have a washed up ex-football star turned construction worker—much like those brothers she always complained about—with her tonight. Was it because she wanted to get under Desmond's and Lance's skin? Was that what she saw when she looked at him? Dale couldn't figure out any other reason.

But he wasn't going to try to come up with one.

Enjoy the moment, he reminded himself.

After all, he wasn't sure how many more moments like this he would get with her.

He released another satisfied moan as she used her elbows to knead his shoulder muscles.

"You better tell your friend, Cheyenne, to watch out," Dale said. "If you start giving massages, her business will be in trouble."

"Cheyenne isn't worried about any of us stealing business away from her," she said with a chuckle. "She has a ton of loyal clients who are eager for her to get back to business in this area."

"So, do your friends concoct their own hair

and skincare products?" Dale asked.

"Actually, that's the one thing they *didn't* want to learn. When I tried to teach them a few recipes, they said it felt like they were back in high school chemistry class. They didn't pay attention back then, either."

"You all remind me of me and my two buddies, Sam and Ian. We've been tight since elementary school."

"The four of us have been friends since the seventh grade," Nyree said. "Although we've had some epic fights over the years. The worst was when Reesa came to the homecoming dance our junior year wearing the same dress I was wearing, even though she was at the mall when I bought mine."

Dale gasped with exaggerated shock. "She didn't!"

Nyree burst out laughing as she continued to knead his spine. God, but her fingers felt good. She ran the heels of her hands up his back, to his shoulder, then brought them down his arms. When she repeated the move, her breasts brushed against his back, and Dale immediately felt himself growing hard—not the most comfortable state to be in while lying facedown on a massage table.

At that point it didn't even make sense to fight his body's reaction to her. He'd been semi-aroused since the moment she turned around in that flooded bathroom with her thin pink T-shirt clinging to her wet body. Just thinking about the way the fabric molded to her small breasts made his mouth water.

"For a minute today, I thought Reesa and I would have another of those epic fights," Nyree said, knocking his one-track mind back into the present.

Not that it helped the situation growing below his waist.

"Do you…uh…" Dale shifted slightly on the table. "Do you think everything will be okay between you two?"

"It will be," she said as her fingers dug into the rigid muscles at the base of his neck. "As long as the house is ready in time. Don't say anything," she quickly added. "I know how hopeless it is at this point."

"It's not hopeless."

"You're going to suggest Desmond and Lance again, aren't you? I still consider them a last resort."

"You really should have given me the whole story behind your timetable," Dale said.

"Would it have changed anything about the way you've tackled the renovation up to this point?"

Dale shrugged his uber-relaxed shoulders. "I could have put in a few more hours earlier into the project?"

"You already work more hours than you should." Her fingers paused in the middle of her rubdown. "I still don't understand how you can put so much effort into this project when my been busting your ass right alongside me for weeks. Why haven't your friends come by to help?"

"Because—" She started, but then she stopped.

"Because?" Dale prompted.

"Because I told them I'd get it done," Nyree said. "It's what I do. I'm the one who gets things done."

"Stop putting all that pressure on yourself, Nyree. You all have a stake in this business. You shouldn't have to take on everything alone. That's too much stress for anyone to deal with, no matter how kickass you are."

When she didn't respond, Dale looked over his shoulder again. He found her staring at him with a look of such vulnerability it caused him to turn and sit up on the massage table.

"What's wrong?" he asked, fitting his hand against her cheek. He ran his thumb back and forth over her cheekbone in a soft caress.

She leaned more heavily into his palm and closed her eyes. "You're right," she said. "That's exactly what I've been doing."

When she looked up at him, her eyes shone with unshed tears. Alarm burst within his chest.

"Shit, Nyree. How much pressure have you been putting on yourself?"

She sucked in a deep breath and blew it out. "I'm the one who came up with the idea to combine the businesses, so it's up to me to make sure it all goes off without a hitch."

"Who says it's all up to you? It's your friends' spa too."

"Yeah, but I'm the one who bought the house."

"Which means you're taking a bigger financial risk than all of them. Even if they lose a few weeks' worth of appointments, they can recoup that in no time. You took on a mortgage so that your friends could have a place to run their businesses. And you don't think they should have just as much responsibility in making sure it all comes together? Are you kidding me, Nyree?"

"I know, I know," she said. "I'm just so used to taking the lead on everything."

Dale huffed out a laugh. "So I've noticed," he said. "You didn't hesitate to make the first move with me either."

"Too bad you're too stubborn to give into me," she murmured.

She turned her head and kissed the center of his palm, and Dale's groin immediately pulled in the most erotically sensual way. The bolt of attraction that had flashed between them from the very first moment he met her exploded.

"Maybe you should try again," he said.

The barrier of the sheet she'd pulled over him, along with his boxer briefs, were no match for the erection that had sprung up in his lap. His body was primed and ready, had been anticipating it for weeks.

He was ready to make things between them

own flesh and blood refuse to take it seriously."

"Easy," he said. "It's because you're working hard to see your dream come true and I don't want to see anything get in the way of that."

"Even though you've only known me a little over a month?" she asked, resuming the massage.

"It's the quality of the time I've known you, not quantity," Dale countered. He looked up at her over his shoulder. "I'm serious, Nyree. I'm amazed at how kickass you are. Some people are too afraid to even admit what they really want to do with their lives. You haven't only admitted it, but you're doing all you can to make it happen. You deserve to see your dream come true."

Her eyes softened and her lips tilted up in a shy smile. "Thank you," she said.

"You're not perfect, though." He resumed his prone position on the table and settled his face in the face cradle.

The kneading stopped again. "Excuse me?"

"You're not perfect," he repeated, raising his head from the cradle. "No one is. So what if the house isn't ready when you said it would be ready? I know your friends have a lot riding on this, but it's not the end of the world if you open a few weeks later than planned."

"Yes, it is," she said. "It could ruin Reesa, Cheyenne and Amara's businesses."

"If there's so much at stake for them, why haven't I seen them at the house sooner? You've something more, something *real*.

He was ready to make her his.

"Come here," Dale said, his voice hoarse with want.

Nyree stepped into the place he'd made for her between his spread legs and wrapped her arms around him. She ran her hands up his back, her oil-slick palms gliding across his skin. He stepped down from the massage table and pulled at the hem of her T-shirt, his lips moving from hers just long enough to pull the fabric from over her head.

Dale considered himself pretty good at foreplay, but he didn't give a shit about foreplay at that moment. He'd been waiting for this to happen for weeks. Foreplay would have to wait for another day.

He unbuckled her shorts and pulled them down her shapely legs, pressing a kiss to her right hip as he made his way down. After she kicked the shorts away, he grabbed her by the waist and lifted her onto the massage table. She braced her hands on either side of her, her legs falling open.

Dale took a moment to just stare at her. She looked amazing in her matching bra and panties. Simple cotton, just as he'd observed underneath her wet t-shirt earlier in the day, but these were blue instead of white. The pale blue fabric looked glorious against her light brown skin.

He slid his palms up her inner thighs, spanning his fingers over her flesh. Then he returned to her mouth, dipping his tongue in and out, loving the taste and texture and heat he found inside.

But her mouth wasn't the only thing he wanted to kiss. And now that he had her in position, he was ready to do every wicked thing he'd fantasized about doing to her over the past few weeks.

With one last deep kiss, Dale tore his mouth from hers and dropped to his knees.

"What...what are you doing?" she asked. Her voice sounded breathless.

He looked up at her from his position on the floor, his eyes intense. "You have to ask?"

He hooked his fingers on the sides of her panties and tugged, urging her to lift up so he could pull them over her hips and down her legs. He grabbed hold of her calves and brought her legs over his shoulders, drawing her closer until she was at the edge of the massage table.

Dale's mouth watered in anticipation. Using both thumbs, he spread her open and swept his tongue up her center in a long, slow swipe. Then he repeated it. Over and over and over again. He increased the pressure, then pulled back, lingering in the midst of her sweetness before bringing her close to the edge again.

Damn. He could do this all night.

Even with the hard-on raging painfully inside his boxer briefs. Even with his busted up knee aching like a bitch as he maintained his crouch. Dale still didn't want to stop. He was so turned on by the way her body responded to him. She was so incredibly wet. And the soft mewls coming from deep in her throat were sexy as hell.

He had nothing he could give her that she couldn't already get for herself. Except this. This was the one way he could prove he was worthy of her.

"Oh, my god, Dale, please," she begged. She clasped his head and lifted her pelvis, holding him against her center.

Dale drilled his tongue inside her as his fingers plucked at her clit, rolling it into a tight bud, then flicking his thumbnail back and forth over it in rapid succession.

Nyree's thighs trembled against his face. Her breath hitched.

"Oh, my god! Oh, my god!" she screamed as she shattered apart against his tongue.

Dale licked up every drip. He had never tasted anything more amazing than her unbelievably sensual flavor.

Grimacing from the pain in his knee, he managed to push himself up from the floor and took her into his arms. She was feather-light as he carried her down the apartment's short hallway and into her bedroom.

It was a mess, with clothes and shoes strewn everywhere, and the bed unmade.

He loved her for it.

It showed him that she wasn't perfect. She was real.

And, for the night, she was his.

"Tell me you have a condom."

Nyree knelt before him on her mattress as Dale stood at the foot of her bed. The erection tenting his black boxer briefs intimidated the hell out of her, but she'd never been one to back down from a challenge. After the amazing journey he'd taken her on with his tongue, she was eager to see just what else he had planned.

"You don't have any?" he asked her.

She pulled her bottom lip between her teeth and shook her head. With the way she'd been pursuing him, why wouldn't he think she was prepared?

"It's, uh, been a while," she said. "And with the way you've been playing hard to get, I wasn't sure anything would ever happen."

He caught her chin between his thumb and forefinger and lifted her face. "I'm happy you're so damn determined," he said before placing a light kiss on her lips.

He left the room and, a minute later, returned with the jeans he'd taken off in her bathroom before his massage. He pulled his wallet from the back pocket and pulled out two condoms.

"This will get us started," he said.

Lust raced through Nyree's bloodstream at the seductive promise in his voice. When he hooked his thumbs in the side of his briefs and pushed them down his hips, she nearly choked.

He was big. As in a lot bigger than anyone else she'd ever been with. Admittedly, that count was relatively low for someone her age. One boy in high school, one in college and Calvin.

She held her hands up. "Um, okay, let's just get this out in the open."

He stopped in the middle of opening the condom. "What's wrong?" His eyes went wide. "Wait, you're not a virgin, are you?"

"No," Nyree said.

Relief flashed across his face. "Thank God. With Desmond and Lance as your older brothers, I wouldn't be surprised if they'd made you wear a chastity belt."

A nervous giggle bubbled up from her chest. "You have no idea how close that is to the truth."

"Oh, I think I have a pretty good idea." Dale pulled the latex from the foil. "I'd have done the same thing if you were my little sister." He looked up from where he'd been concentrating on rolling the condom over his erection. "Erase what I just said. That sounded weird as hell."

"A little," Nyree said with another giggle. Goodness, she had to stop that. She wasn't even a giggler.

She let out a deep breath. "I, um, I just need you to take this slow. You're big. And I'm…not. And, like I said, it's been a while."

His face softened as he walked up to her. He captured her cheek in his palm and pressed his lips to hers. "It's been a while for me too," he said. "I'm not going to hurt you, Nyree. I promise."

His promise was sweet, but it wouldn't reduce the size of him. Nyree tried to relax, knowing it would be easier if she released some of the tension flowing through her.

Dale urged her to lie back on the bed, following her down onto the mattress. He levered himself up on one arm and, with his other hand, gently urged her thighs to part. Even though she was still wet from her orgasm, he sucked two of his fingers into his mouth, coating them before reaching down again and prodding her flesh. Sensations flooded her, stirring deep within her belly and branching out to every extremity.

"Tell me if I need to pull back," he whispered against her cheek.

Nyree locked onto his wrist and pressed down, urging him to push deeper.

He complied, nestling his fingers inside her, moving slowly, until they were fully embedded. His fingers started to move in a circular motion, and Nyree was certain she would melt then and there. She fisted her hands in the sheets, pulling her bottom lip between her teeth to hush the whimpers that she couldn't seem to control.

She turned to liquid as Dale continued his sensual play. Their gazes locked, his eyes heavy with heat and something...else. Something that touched her very soul. It was the intensity she saw in his face, as if her pleasure was the most important thing in his world.

When his thumb joined in the action, brushing against her tender clit, she was hit with a wave of pleasure so intense her back bowed off the bed.

"Can we just do this all night?" she moaned.

"It gets a lot better," Dale said.

And then he proceeded to show her. When he dipped his head and captured her nipple between his lips, Nyree thought she would surely die. She wasn't equipped to handle the multitude of sensations spiraling through her. He tongued the sensitive nub, swirling his tongue around the tip of her breast, grazing it with his teeth. He sucked gently, then increased the pressure, while at the same time increasing the rhythm of his thrusting fingers.

Her breath hitched, and the cry she'd tried to hold back escaped from her throat.

"I told you it gets better," Dale murmured against her breast.

Nyree locked her legs around his waist. "I...want you...inside me," she choked out.

"Not as much as I want to be there."

After hooking his arm around her hip, he reached down between them and grasped his cock, then guided it inside her.

"Relax," Dale said on a gasp.

Nyree made a concerted effort to release the

anxiety flowing through her, and as he sank in by gentle degrees, her body gradually began to welcome him. He stretched her deliciously wide, pulling out, then pushing in with slow, deliberate thrusts. His back was still slick from the oil she'd used during his massage. It made it even easier to run her fingers up and down his spine. She dug her fingers into his shoulders, holding on for dear life as he finally drove himself completely inside of her. Never had she felt so full, so incredibly, marvelously full.

"You okay?" Dale whispered against her cheek.

She nodded. "Soooo okay."

"Okay is good, but not good enough." He moved his hips, rocking slowly at first, then picking up the pace. "I need you to be better than just okay."

He lunged until her inner thighs burned with the exquisite ache of having to open so wide for him. She wrapped her arms around his neck and held on, moving with him, tilting her hips up to meet his thrusts.

"Faster," she cried. "Please, go faster."

He obliged, placing his hands on either side of her head and working his hips like a piston, pumping in and out, over and over and over. Dale wet his fingers again, reached down between them and rubbed her clit, even as he continued to move within her.

One touch and Nyree's orgasm hit out of nowhere, hurtling her into the sweetest oblivion she'd ever experienced. Dale's hips surged once, twice and then a third time before he erupted, his limbs shaking as he came with raging force. He wrapped his arm around her, holding her pelvis to his as his hips gave one last desperate thrust.

He pulled out and collapsed onto her bed, his deep breaths soughing in and out.

"Ten years later, and I'm still getting knocked out by a Grant."

Nyree burst out laughing. "I hope this knockout was better than what you experienced with the other two Grants."

"A thousand times better."

"And just think, we still have another condom."

His laughter rumbled from deep within his chest. "That's the best damn news in the world, isn't it?"

He reached over and scooped his arm underneath her, then urged her to climb on top of him. He pressed a kiss to her lips before pulling his head back slightly and staring into her eyes.

"Did I hurt you?"

Nyree shook her head. "I may need a little breather before we put that other condom to use, but I'm okay."

Dale reached over and grabbed a dirty sock from her floor. Using the sock, he pulled the condom from his still semi-erect cock, balled it up, and tossed it on her nightstand.

"Really?" she asked.

"What?"

"You just stuffed a condom in a sock like a teenager trying to hide the evidence."

"Actually, like someone whose legs are too weak to get up and go to the bathroom to clean up," he said.

"Remind me that's over there," she said. "I sometimes bring my laundry over to my mom's. That's a conversation I never want to have."

That deep laugh rumbled in his chest again. "Awkward with a capital A?"

"All caps and ten exclamation points."

Dale folded his arms underneath his head. "You seem to spend a lot of time there," he said. "Whenever I text you, you're either on your way to your mom's or just leaving."

She shrugged. "Habit. I've only been in this apartment for a year. Honestly, I was afraid to leave home."

His brows spiked. "Afraid to leave home? You?" Dale shook his head. "I don't believe that. Doesn't go with your personality."

"I guess 'afraid' isn't the right word. Anxious, maybe? I wasn't sure how my mom and grandmother would get along without me there." She folded her hands on his chest and rested her chin on the backs of her fingers. "My grandmother had a stroke a couple of years ago, not too long after aunt Hazel died. My mom spends a lot of time taking care of her. Having to attend to the house, as well as my grandmother, is a lot for her to handle.

"Not to mention taking care of Lance and Desmond. I wasn't joking when I said they aren't capable of feeding themselves, or doing their own laundry. That's why I'm often there, helping her to get it all done."

Dale pushed a strand of curly hair from her face, tucking it behind her ear. "Your brothers are grown men. It's not your responsibility to take care of them."

"I know." She shrugged. "But I've been doing it for so long that it comes as second nature. I rarely see it as taking care of them, but more as helping out my mom."

"I think it's just in your nature to be everything for everybody. But you do realize you can't live your life that way, right, Nyree?"

She nodded.

"But it doesn't change how you feel about the renovation, does it?" he asked.

"No," she said. "When it comes to the house, it still falls on my shoulders." She looked up at him. "I know it isn't realistic, but I want you to be straight with me, Dale. Is there any way we can still get it completed in time?"

"I'm going to get it done," he said. "If I have to work around the clock, I'll figure out a way to do it."

Her heart melted then and there.

But Nyree also knew it wasn't completely fair. She'd brought this chaos upon herself. If she'd been more forthcoming, if she'd been honest with the girls back when Desmond and Lance first pulled out of the job, they could have put some contingency plans in place.

"What about your football tutoring thing?" she asked. "You'll still need time for that, right?"

"Yeah," he said with a weary sigh.

She caught the apprehension that flashed across his features. "What?" Nyree asked.

His full lips twisted up in a frown. "I found out that Kendrick—the kid I've been working with—has someone doing his schoolwork for him. He probably has several people doing his work for him." He looked down at her, his eyes searing with raw honesty. "At least, I did back when I was in school."

Nyree shook her head. "You mean to tell me that's still happening?"

"Your brothers too, right?"

"Of course," she said. "Desmond graduated high school with a 3.0 average. Don't get me wrong, as much as I complain about them, I do love my brothers, but do you really think Desmond earned a 3.0 GPA in high school?"

"Yeah, well, it wasn't just high school for me. It happened in college, too."

He closed his eyes, the corners pinching with his pained grimace. When he opened them again, the frank sadness and shame staring back at her stole Nyree's breath.

"I have a college degree that isn't worth the paper it's written on," he confessed. "My professors were all too happy to give me a bunch of grades I didn't earn. All I had to do was show up for class and I got a B-plus."

His shame was palpable. It made her ache for him.

"You can't shoulder all the blame for that," Nyree said as she ran her palm along his side in a comforting caress. "You were young. And that sounds like a young college student's dream."

"I loved it," he said. "Can you imagine what my life was like back then? Big man on campus. Didn't have to worry about anything but performing on the field and going to frat parties. It was heaven."

He shook his head. "I was so damn stupid." He looked down at her again. "I've never regretted anything as much as I regret not actually earning my degree."

"You can always go back," she said.

Dale's gaze jerked to hers. He looked at her as if she'd spoken in a foreign language.

"What?" Nyree asked. "People go back to school all the time. I plan to eventually go back to get a degree in business."

"Business?"

She nodded. "I have a head for chemistry, but if I'm going to build my product line into a global empire, I'll need to learn how to actually run a business."

"My degree is in business," Dale said with a humorless grunt. "If I'd paid attention in class we could have formed a partnership."

She pressed a kiss to his bare chest. "We can

go to business school together," she teased.

"Nah." Dale shook his head. "If I went back I'd go into teaching, so that I could coach high school football."

Nyree cupped her chin in her palm. "I think you'd make a fantastic high school coach. You should do it."

"I don't know about that." He huffed out a sigh. "But, first, I need to figure out what to do about Kendrick."

Nyree frowned. "Is there a question about what you should do? It seems obvious to me."

"It's not so cut and dry, Nyree. I don't want to be the person who ruins the kid's chances. It could stop him from getting into a Division One school if I expose him."

"That's not what's important here."

"It is to Kendrick. Who am I to dictate what should be important to him? Maybe he *will* make it to the pros. Is it really fair for me to transfer all my shit onto him? Just because it came back to bite me in the ass, who says it won't work out for Kendrick?"

"History says it," Nyree argued. "Making it onto an NFL roster is one of the hardest feats anyone can ever accomplish, and you know it. I don't have to school you on the number of young boys from this area who have had their football dreams crushed."

"That's just it. Kendrick can make it. If he works hard enough, he's good enough to be one of those one-in-a-million shots to make it to the

NFL."

"Even if he does make it to the NFL, is it really worth giving up an education? One game, one play can change his entire life." Nyree sat up in bed, pulling the sheet up to cover her breasts. "How would you feel if a few years from now, you're sitting at home on a Sunday afternoon, watching Kendrick play ball and he's suddenly blindsided? With that one hit, you know his career is over. And that life is going to be harder for him because you didn't speak up for him?

"Better yet, think about it this way," she said. "How much do you wish that someone had spoken up for *you* when your coaches and professors where handing you everything on a silver platter?"

Nyree knew she'd hit her mark when she saw the pain that slashed across Dale's face. She reached over and caressed his arm with soothing strokes, trying to wipe away the sting of her words.

"I know it's hard. No one wants to be seen as the bad guy, but sometimes being the bad guy is a good thing, Dale."

He took her hand and placed a kiss at the center of her palm. "Wise words," he said.

She gave her bare shoulders a sexy little shake and winked at him. "I'm full of them."

"Thanks for listening," he said. "I appreciate it." He released another of those heavy sighs. "I guess I have a decision to make."

Nyree leaned forward and placed a kiss on

his lips. "The only decision that needs to be made right now is who's going to be on top." She straddled his lap. "And I just made it."

Chapter Eight

Dale stood with his arms crossed, his feet braced apart, a whistle perched on the edge of his lips. His head moved from left to right and back again as he watched Kendrick run 4 x 4 sprints across the trampled grass.

"You look like a football coach."

Dale's head whipped around. Ian stood just a few yards behind him. He'd been thinking so much about the dilemma he faced with Kendrick's cheating that he hadn't even heard his friend walk up.

Dale noticed the tension around Ian's mouth, and didn't have to ask what brought him here.

He did anyway.

"Charlie?"

Ian nodded. "The director at the hospice facility called them about an hour ago."

Dale dropped his head. "Shit," he whispered. "Give me a minute to wrap up."

"No." Ian shook his head. "Sam asked us not to come."

"And we're going to listen to him?" Dale asked.

"I think he's good," Ian said. "His mom is

there, and his sister is on her way down from Atlanta."

"I guess they're honoring Charlie's wish and not holding a funeral?" Dale asked.

"Yeah. No funeral, no memorial." Ian hunched his shoulders. "It's what he wanted." Ian gestured his chin toward Kendrick. "How are things going here?"

"Don't ask," Dale said.

"From the looks of it he seems fast, especially for a guy his size." A smile hitched up the corner of his mouth. "Reminds me of you during your time on the field."

"Yeah, he reminds me of me, too," Dale said. "In more ways than one."

"I need to get going. I have to swing by Kiera's Catering. Sonny had the crew over there whip up some dinner for Sam's family."

"That girlfriend—I'm sorry, that *wife*—of yours is something special, man."

"She's cute, too," Ian said with a smile that didn't reach his eyes. Dale figured his friend was struggling to hold it together in the same way that he was with the news of Charlie passing.

"I'll shoot Sam a text in a little bit, just to make sure he's doing okay," Dale said. He put a hand out for Ian. "Thanks for coming over to tell me."

Ian caught his hand and pulled him in for a one-arm hug. He gestured to the whistle hanging from a string around Dale's neck.

"Put a Maplesville Mustang ball cap on your

head and you're one of the coaches," Ian said. He squeezed his hand. "You can do this, Dale. You're practically doing it right now."

Once Ian left, Dale turned back to Kendrick, who'd finished his sprints and was now running through a four-corners drill, shuffling from one orange cone to another. Dale showed him how to keep his form, even when bending to touch the top of the cones, then instructed him to start again from the beginning.

When he caught Lowell Robertson's espresso-brown Mercedes out of the corner of his eye, Dale's stomach began to churn. He peered slightly over his shoulder, watching the car pull up to the edge of the open field where they were practicing.

His eyes fell shut as his thoughts went back and forth, toiling over just what he should do about Kendrick's cheating. He mentally cursed the kid for allowing him to find out. Dale would have been better off never knowing.

But Kendrick wouldn't be better off. *That* was the issue.

And now that Dale knew about it, he had to speak up. He couldn't allow what had happened to him to happen to this kid.

"How's it going out here?" Lowell greeted, clamping his palm on Dale's shoulder.

"He's looking good. We just ran through conditioning drills, and his reaction time has improved by point eight seconds."

Kendrick ran over to them. "My 40-yard

dash was 4.89," he said. "That's better than that guy from Southern Cal did at the NFL combine."

A huge smile spread across Lowell Robertson's face. "Speaking of Southern Cal," he said. "I just got off the phone with the defensive coordinator there. He's coming down to interview for a job with Mississippi State, and he wants to meet with you."

Dale's head jerked back. "It's a little early for him to talk to recruiters, isn't it?"

"Not in my book," Lowell said.

"What about his college entrance exams? He'll need to get those behind him before he can start talking to recruiters."

"Don't worry about that," Lowell said. "I've got that covered." He pointed at Kendrick. "Remind me to get the photo from that kid so I can upload it to the testing center's site." He huffed out a laugh, returning his attention to Dale. "They're getting pretty strict with this test security."

Dale just stood there, dumbfounded. Dumbfounded and disgusted.

"So you know about his cheating," he said to Kendrick's father.

Kendrick let out a sigh. "Man, would you get off of this? I told you not to worry about it."

"My son is right," Lowell said, his earlier smile nowhere to be seen. "It's none of your business. I hired you to train him on the football field. That's it."

Dale shook his head. He couldn't believe

what he was hearing.

Back when he was getting everything handed to him in high school and college, his biggest fear was having his parents or Vanessa find out about it. Even now, years later, he was ashamed to admit to both his family and his friends that he'd allowed others to cheat for him in school.

Not only did Lowell Robertson know about it, but he was aiding in his own son's cheating.

Dale turned to Kendrick.

"Don't do this to yourself," Dale cautioned. "Don't let people use you, because that's what this is, Kendrick. They're using you on the football field, but they don't give a shit about you."

"That's enough!" Lowell said.

"Even your own damn father doesn't give a shit about you," Dale continued. "Paying someone to take a test for you isn't looking out for you, and it's not love. It's using you to get what he wants."

"Get the hell away from my son," Robertson said, stepping in front of Kendrick. "And you can forget about me investing in your contractor business."

Dale folded his arms over his chest. "If that means your son will actually get an education instead of spending the next four years being someone's workhorse on the football field, then it's worth it."

Hell, he wasn't going to take Robertson's

money anyway. Dale had already decided that starting his own general contractor business wasn't part of the future he saw for himself.

"Let's get out of here," Lowell said. He pointed at Dale. "If you say anything about this test, we're going to deny it, and we're going to make sure you don't get near a football field again."

"You can take your threat and shove it up your ass," Dale said.

The look on Lowell's face could freeze boiling water, but Dale didn't give a shit. He couldn't believe he'd been worried about whether he should tell the man about his son's cheating. Not only did Robertson know about it, he'd *sanctioned* it.

Dale ran both hands down his face, pulling in deep breaths and letting them out slowly. He stood there for a full ten minutes after Kendrick and Lowell left, contemplating what his next step should be. The odds that the coaching staff at Magnolia Bend High School knew nothing about Kendrick's cheating were slim. He wouldn't be surprised if the coaches and Lowell were working together.

"Damn, this day sucks," he whispered.

Between learning of Charlie's passing and Lowell Robertson's complicity in his own son's cheating, Dale didn't know whether he wanted to punch a wall or drink an entire bottle of whiskey.

No, what he *really* wanted to do was drive to

Lakeshore Refinery, bust through the doors of the lab department, toss Nyree over his shoulder caveman style and carry her off to bed. If anything could get his mind off his troubles, it was being with Nyree. Over the past two weeks, when he wasn't working at the Whitmer House, he was with her in bed. Or in the shower. Or on her massage table.

But it was about more than the sex. So much more. Just holding her hand while they watched television was enough to put his mind at ease and warm him from the inside out.

Dale smiled to himself.

It didn't take a college degree to figure out that he was in love with her. He never thought he could fall for someone so damn fast, but there was no denying it. He'd fallen hard.

He'd fallen *so* hard that he was ready to do whatever he had to do to convince her that he was worthy of her.

He sobered as he accepted another truth. The truth that he was also prepared to lose her. Because the one thing that meant even more to him than having Nyree for himself was making sure she got to see her dream come true. And in order to make that happen, he would have to do the one thing she'd told him she didn't want to do.

Cursing under his breath, he picked up the orange cones and tossed them in the bed of his truck. Then he slid behind the wheel, turned over the ignition and headed west toward St.

Pierre.

Nyree trudged up the stairs to her apartment, cursing her supervisors for asking her to cover yet another shift at the last minute. What was the point of saving up so many of her vacation days if the lab could call her in at the drop of a hat?

"They'd better not call again," Nyree said as she opened her door and walked into her bare apartment. Most of her things had been moved into the Whitmer House, but Nyree knew better than to go there right now. She wouldn't get a wink of sleep, not with the way Dale had been working around the clock to get the house ready.

She felt guilty not being there right alongside him, but it couldn't be helped. She wasn't in a position to ignore the lab when they called. She needed her day job to help pay the mortgage on the Whitmer House until her product line started turning a profit. Reesa, Cheyenne and Amara were all paying her rent, but she'd charged them the bare minimum. After all, her friends didn't have a second income. She did.

And as much as she bellyached about the lab, Nyree recognized how blessed she was to have her job and to be on the verge of opening her own business.

Still, right then, she wanted nothing more

than a hot shower and at least six hours of uninterrupted sleep. She'd have to settle for two. She'd promised Dale she would be at the house no later than 9:00 a.m. They had less than a week to go before Any Way You Want It's grand opening.

"Stop fooling yourself," Nyree said as she pulled on an oversized t-shirt and curled up on her sofa. She tugged the afghan her grandmother had crocheted for her years ago up to her chin and fought back her disappointment over the reality she'd been forced to accept.

The house wouldn't be ready by this coming Saturday.

They'd been lucky to discover that they wouldn't have to change out all of the plumbing. One of Dale's coworkers from Harding Construction came over a couple of days earlier to run a test, and was able to pinpoint the weak spot. It had only taken them one day to fix it and repair the wall. But it was a day they didn't have to spare.

While she lay in bed with Dale the morning before, he'd given her his honest take. They would need a miracle in order to finish the house on time. She'd prayed for one, but Nyree wasn't expecting any miracles.

And she only had herself to blame.

If she had swallowed her pride and gone to Desmond and Lance, there would have been a chance that they could complete the renovations in time for the grand opening she'd planned, but

Nyree refused to give Desmond the pleasure of saying 'I told you so' or looking at her with that smug smile.

"This stubborn pride will be the death of you," Nyree whispered.

Thankfully, according to Dale, the house should be completed by next Tuesday, a week from today. That would give them time to have everything in place for the wedding party Amara had booked, so at least her friends' businesses wouldn't suffer because of Nyree's hardheadedness.

But she wouldn't be able to honor her Aunt Hazel on her birthday.

The realization gutted her. Without the money her aunt had left her, Nyree wouldn't have been able to afford the down payment on the Whitmer House and there would be no Any Way You Want It Salon and Spa.

"Maybe there's still a chance," Nyree said.

Ignoring the bitter taste that instantly formed on her tongue at the thought of what she was about to do, Nyree jumped up from the sofa and raced over to the counter where she'd left her phone to charge. She brought up Desmond's number, but hesitated before pressing the touchscreen.

Nyree slumped against the kitchen counter.

"What's the point? It's too late now."

And it wasn't as if she expected them to walk off in the middle of a job anyway. It was different a couple of months ago, when she'd told Desmond about needing to push up the timetable for the work on the Whitmer House. He and Lance had just finished a job and hadn't yet started on the next one.

Nyree thought about Lance's visit a few weeks earlier. If she hadn't been so damn stubborn.

"You made your own bed with this one," she said.

Her phone chimed with an incoming text. She looked at the message from Dale and laughed.

You'd better be sleeping. Meet me at the house when you wake up.

Just as she set the phone down, another text message came through.

Don't hate me for being the bad guy. I did what I had to do.

"What?" Nyree said. What in the heck was he talking about?

She called him, but the phone went straight to voicemail.

Well, she could forget sleep, not with the dozen questions swirling around her head after that text message.

Nyree changed into a t-shirt and a pair of jeans, and in less than five minutes, was on her way to Maplesville. When she turned onto Silver Oak Drive, she slowly let her foot off the gas pedal as she drew nearer to Whitmer House.

"What the hell?" Nyree murmured.

The place was abuzz with activity.

Cheyenne and Amara were in the front yard, planting flower bulbs along the brick-laid walkway leading to the front door. A guy Nyree didn't recognize stood on the colonnade with a pressure washer, cleaning the black and green mold from one of the columns. She could see the stark difference between those he'd cleaned already and those still left to be pressure washed.

Nyree stomped on the brakes when she caught sight of Desmond and Lance carrying her Aunt Hazel's salon chair from the back of a trailer.

"What in the hell?"

She parked on the curb behind a shiny black-and-chrome motorcycle.

"Hey," Cheyenne said as Nyree climbed out of her SUV. "Didn't you just get off work? You should be sleeping."

"What are you guys doing here?" Nyree asked.

"What does it look like?" Lance called as he and Desmond passed by with the chair.

Cheyenne rolled her eyes. "Your brother is an ass."

"Yet you're seeing him, aren't you?" Nyree asked.

Cheyenne shrugged. "He's a good lay. But he's still an ass."

Nyree cupped her palms over her ears. "I don't want to hear this."

"Oh, grow up," Cheyenne said.

Nyree ignored her. She turned to Amara. "What are you all doing here?" she asked again.

Amara stood and dusted the dirt off her hands. "This is our business too," her friend said. "We never should have let you take on all of this by yourself."

"You just make it so damn easy to leave it up to you," Cheyenne said. "Because you *always* handle everything."

"But you shouldn't have to," Amara said. "Reesa had a couple of early clients, but she'll be here by the afternoon. We're going to get this house ready to open by this weekend, and it's going to be as amazing as we all envisioned when we used to sit around Hazel's shop all those years ago."

Nyree was in danger of choking on the emotion welling up in her throat.

"I would hug you two right now if you both weren't so filthy," she said with a shaky laugh.

"You'd better get down here in the dirt with us," Cheyenne said. "You don't want the wrath of Dale the Cute Ass Construction Worker coming down on your head."

"Is that my official title?"

Nyree turned at the sound of the deep voice just behind her.

"You did this?" she asked him.

Dale nodded. He tipped his head, motioning for her to follow him. They walked over to the huge oak tree that shaded the right side of the front lawn.

Nyree folded her arms across her chest. "So, you went behind my back and got my brothers to help out?"

"Don't ask me to apologize for it, because I won't," he said, matching her pose.

He looked a lot more intimidating than she probably did, so she straightened her shoulders. "Even after I specifically told you that I didn't want them involved?" she asked.

"You also told me that you wanted this house done by the fourth. You couldn't have it both ways."

"So you took it upon yourself to choose for me? Is that it?"

A muscle ticked in his jaw. "You're the one who said that being the bad guy is sometimes a good thing. Well, I decided this was one of those times." His voice was heavy with resolve. "Even if it means losing you."

Tension thickened the air as they stood there staring at each other.

It finally broke when Nyree threw her arms around him and said, "Just shut up and kiss me."

She brought her hands up to his face and tugged his head down to meet her lips. Dale caressed her back before bringing his palms to rest on her hips.

"I just couldn't bare the thought of you not opening on your aunt's birthday," he whispered against her lips. "I know how much it means to you."

"Thank you for refusing to allow my stubbornness to get in the way of it happening. *And* for going behind my back. Just try not to make a habit of it."

"These were desperate times," he said. "I had to do what I had to do."

Nyree tipped her head toward the house. "How did you convince those two to help?"

"I basically told them they needed to man-up and help out their little sister, because you've spent much of your life taking care of them."

Her heart melted the tiniest bit.

"They agreed with me," Dale said. "It was the next part that nearly caused a brawl to break out."

Nyree eyed him wearily. "What happened?"

He shrugged. "I told them that they needed to get over the fact that you're with me, because I like what the two of us have going, and I plan on being with you for however long you'll have me."

Well, there went the rest of her heart, melting like a snow cone within her chest.

He stared into her eyes, his gaze intense. "Look, Nyree, I know you can do better than me —"

"Don't," she said. "Don't ever say those words. Don't even *think* them." She pressed a fierce kiss to his lips. "You are so much more than I could have ever hoped for, Dale. How can you not see that?"

"You still think so? Even after what I told

you about what I did in college?"

"And as I told you, you were young and impressionable. You tell me what college kid wouldn't have done the same thing if they'd been in your position? Our mistakes don't make us who we are, Dale. What we learn from them, how we grow from them—that's what's important."

Nyree's shoulders slumped with a resigned sigh. "That's why I'll have to suck it up and apologize to those brothers of mine for behaving like a bratty little sister instead of an adult these past couple of months."

"Nah." Dale shook his head. "The youngest reserves the right to be a brat sometimes."

"Spoken like someone who knows a thing or two about being the youngest," she said with a laugh. She kissed him again, because she couldn't help herself. "How could you possibly think you were ever in danger of losing me?" she asked. "I'm the luckiest person I know, finding a man as funny and kind and giving as you are." Her mouth tipped up in a smile. "And did I mention sexy?"

"Sexy is important," Dale said.

"Very important."

She caressed his jaw. "Thank you," Nyree said.

"You already thanked me."

"I'm thanking you again."

"For what?"

"For being who you are. For believing in my

dream and going out of your way to help make it come true. For everything."

"It's my pleasure," he said, placing the gentlest kiss upon her lips. He touched his forehead to hers and stared into her eyes. "So, are we good?" Dale asked.

She nodded. "We're more than good. We're perf—" Dale's brow rose. "We're great," she amended.

Although, in her mind, it was absolutely perfect.

He kissed her again. "That's good enough for me."

"So, will we have to see this shit whenever you two are around now?" came Desmond's disgusted voice.

Nyree turned to find her brothers standing a couple of feet away, their arms crossed over their chests.

"Get used to it," Dale said, tightening his hold on her.

"I really hate this, you know?" Desmond said as he walked over to them. "But I love you, so I'll deal with it."

"Not as if you had a choice," Nyree said, disengaging from Dale's hold and wrapping her arms around her brother. "But I love your big meathead, too. Thanks for coming over," she said. She turned to Lance and hugged him. "I'm sorry I was too stubborn to accept your help sooner."

"We should have been here from the

beginning," Lance said. He gestured toward Desmond. "Blame him."

"No more blaming anyone. There's too much work to do to waste any more time on that kind of nonsense," Nyree said as she grabbed Dale's hand.

Desmond looked at their clasped hands and frowned. He brought his eyes back up to Dale. "You're still an asshole who made a bitch move in that game." Then he turned and started for the house.

Lance just shook his head, but before following Desmond, he put his hand out for Dale, who clasped it in a firm handshake.

Once her brothers had left, Dale peered down at her and said, "Well, family gatherings will be fun."

Nyree burst out laughing.

A cute vintage VW Beetle pulled up to the curb, and the guy who'd been pressure washing the columns jogged over to it. "Oh, hell yeah," he called out. "Ladies and gents, it's time to refuel."

"That's my friend, Ian," Dale explained. "And the knockout carrying the tray of cupcakes is his wife, Sonny."

"Can she bake?"

"Better than anyone I know."

"Well, let's go and get us some cupcakes. Then we're getting this house done. Any Way You Want It will be open for business by this weekend."

Carrying two mugs of coffee from the kitchen, Dale couldn't help the satisfied smile that traveled across his lips as he stepped over the trail of forgotten clothes he and Nyree had left on his bedroom floor. He shoved his steel-toe boots under the bed, but left Nyree's black lace panties and red bra right where she'd tossed them.

"Two sugars and one cream," he said, handing her the mug.

"Thank you." She shoved the hair from her face. Her sleepy smile was one of the sexiest sights he'd ever laid eyes on. He'd worn her out last night, and he didn't regret a single second of it.

He settled back against the headboard, and with his free hand, hooked an arm around her waist and pulled her to his side. He couldn't get enough of the feel of her warm skin against him.

"It's too bad you have to use so much of your vacation time getting things ready for the grand opening this weekend," Dale said. "I'd love to keep you in bed until Monday."

"That would be nice, wouldn't it?" she said with a laugh. She sipped her coffee. "Oh, this is good."

Her sexy moan drizzled down his spine like warm honey.

"However, as much as I'd love to spend the

weekend in bed with you, I don't want to miss a minute of Any Way You Want It's grand opening. And not because I want to control everything," she added quickly. "My girls and I have all wanted this for so long. I just want to be there to celebrate with them."

"You deserve to enjoy it," Dale said, pressing a kiss to her forehead.

"You, sir, deserve some enjoyment yourself for all you did to make this happen. Which is why I'm going to give you another of my special massages as soon as I'm done with this coffee."

Dale promptly grabbed the mug from her hand and placed both his and hers on the side table next to the bed. Nyree squealed as he picked her up and twisted her around, until she lay flat on her back. Just as he zeroed in on her neck, there was a knock on the front door.

He looked at the time on the alarm clock next to his bed. "Who in the hell would be here this early in the morning?"

"Well, go see who it is." Nyree shoved at his chest.

"Shit." He pushed himself up from the bed and pulled on the jeans he'd left at the foot of it last night. Due to his body's overly excited anticipation of what the knock at the door had interrupted, he had the hardest time tugging the zipper up.

Dale cursed all the way to his front door, but when he opened it he stopped short.

"Kendrick?"

"Hey," the teen murmured, then immediately dropped his eyes to his feet, which he shuffled from side to side. "I'm, umm, sorry it's so early. I wanted to stop by before school."

Dale thought about inviting him in, then remembered the naked woman in his bed. Instead, he stepped outside onto the small porch, leaving the door slightly ajar behind him.

"What's up?" Dale asked.

"I, uh, was thinking about what you said during our final session. About how people used to take your tests for you and stuff?"

Dale crossed his arms over his bare chest. "Yeah. What about it?"

"You never got in trouble, right?"

"Depends on what you mean by trouble. If you're asking if I ever got caught, the answer is no. But it still spelled trouble for me in the long run."

"I can see how it would." Kendrick pulled his bottom lip between his teeth. "I don't want the guy my dad paid to take that test for me. I want to do it on my own. I mean, what if I get to Mississippi State, or LSU, or wherever I end up, and can't keep up in my classes?" He gestured to Dale. "Or what if I get hurt, like you did?"

"Both are very real possibilities," Dale said. "If I had it to do over again, I'd choose differently." Dale pulled in a deep breath. "Are you okay telling this to your father, or do you want me to be there with you to back you up?"

A smile pulled at Kendrick's lips. "Nah, I

can do it. I'm bigger than he is."

Dale huffed out a laugh. "You're a good kid, Kendrick."

"Thanks." His gaze darted to the side before coming back to Dale. "I'm sorry we won't get to work together anymore. I learned a lot from you. You're a good teacher."

Dale's chest tightened. Emotion clogged his throat. "I'm still willing to teach you."

"Even though my dad won't pay for it?"

"I don't care about the money." Dale said. "Go on to school. We'll figure it all out."

As the teen turned to leave, Dale caught him by the shoulder. "I'm proud of you, Kendrick. I know this wasn't an easy decision."

"It's the right one, though," the teen said.

"Damn right it is."

He stood on the porch and watched as Kendrick walked to the curb and climbed into his pickup truck. Dale leaned his elbows on the porch's railing, ignoring the chipped paint digging into his skin. He covered his face in his hands and pulled in several deep breaths.

"That was interesting."

He whipped around to find Nyree standing in his doorway, wrapped in the dark blue sheet from his bed.

"How much of it did you hear?"

"Enough to know that you are one amazing man," she said. "Offering to continue tutoring him for free? That's incredibly generous."

"Kendrick shouldn't suffer because his dad's

an asshole. Besides, I liked it." He shook his head. "No, I loved it. I loved it so much more than working on any construction site, Nyree."

She walked up to him and caressed his jaw. "Then do it," she said. "If you love it this much, then coaching is what you should be doing. Who cares that you'll have to go back to school to earn a second degree, Dale. People do it all the time. At least you'll know that you've earned this one."

"It scares the hell out of me, but I think you're right."

"From now on let's just take that as a given. It will make things so much easier."

Dale threw his head back with a laugh. "God, I love it when you're being a sassy know-it-all. It's sexy."

"I'll remember to be that way more often," she said with a wink.

"Do you remember what you promised me before that knock at the door?" He tugged at the sheet she clutched to her breasts. "Time to pay up."

Epilogue

Nyree stood on the sidewalk across Silver Maple Drive, staring at the stately white house with lights blazing in the mullioned windows and music streaming in from the opened door. The grand opening party was in full swing, but she'd needed a minute to just take it all in.

Artfully constructed pink and gold balloon bouquets lined the walkway leading up to the front doors of the Whitmer House, now officially known as Any Way You Want It Salon and Spa — not *Anyway* You Want It, which is what the sign she'd ordered for the front lawn read when the installer had come to set it up yesterday. Compared to the other problems they'd faced, not having a sign was nothing.

She reached over and captured Dale's hand, tucking it against her stomach as she continued to marvel at what they'd managed to pull off.

"You know, I'm pretty unstoppable when I put it in my mind to do something, but I have to be honest, for a while there I wasn't sure this would actually happen."

Dale looked at her with mock affront. "How dare you doubt yourself," he said.

She laughed, bringing his hand up and placing a kiss on his fingers. "Silly of me, I know."

A dark blue Volvo pulled up to the curb in front of the house. Vanessa Chauvin got out on the driver's side while a blonde with a short pixie cut climbed out of the passenger seat.

"What are you two doing out here?" Vanessa called to them.

"Just checking out the view," Dale said.

"Go in," Nyree said. "There's plenty of food and free samples of Naturally Nyree beauty products."

"It's a good thing I brought my big purse," Vanessa said. "By the way, this is Tammy. I hope it's okay that I have a plus-one."

"Absolutely," Nyree said.

"We'll see you both inside," Vanessa said with a wave.

Dale looked at his sister's retreating form, his brow arched.

"So?" Nyree asked. "Do you think her plus-one is her—"

"New girlfriend?" Dale asked. "God, I hope so. Maybe she'll keep her nose out of my love life if she finally has one of her own."

"But your love life is so very interesting," she said with a grin.

"It is now," Dale replied, placing a kiss on her lips.

"Come on, Nyree," Reesa called from the front doorway. "It's time to christen the house."

She and Dale made their way across the street and into the house. Reesa, Cheyenne and Amara were standing in the vestibule, lined up in front of her Aunt Hazel's old counter. In Amara's arm was a crystal candy jar filled with bright pink lollipops.

She held the jar out to Nyree. "You do the honors."

Emotion welled in Nyree's throat as she took the candy jar from her friend and held it up in the air—a toast to her aunt.

"To Hazel Elizabeth Mitchell, for making this all possible."

"To Hazel," Reesa said.

"To Hazel," the rest of the crowd chimed in.

With Dale standing behind her, his hands resting gently on her waist, Nyree set the candy jar down on the counter, where it would sit, ready and waiting to satisfy the sweet tooth of Any Way You Want It's guests for years to come.

Thank you so much for purchasing and reading
Any Way You Want It.

Read the entire Moments in Maplesville series:
A Perfect Holiday Fling (Callie & Stefan)
A Little Bit Naughty (Jada & Mason)
Just a Little Taste (Kiera & Trey)
I Dare You! (Stephanie & Dustin)
All You Can Handle (Sonny & Ian)
Any Way You Want It (Nyree & Dale)
Any Time You Need Me (Aubrey & Sam)

The Holmes Brother Series:

Set in New Orleans, the Holmes Brothers series
follows the lives of Elijah, Tobias, and Alexander
Holmes as they find love in one of the world's
most romantic cities.

Read *Deliver Me, Release Me,* and *Rescue Me,*
available both individually and in a special
bundle edition!

In Her Wildest Dreams

Event planner Erica Cole recruits her best friend
to help her plan the ultimate Valentine's Day
fantasy, but chocolatier Gavin Foster is
determined to show her that they should be

more than just friends.

The Rebound Guy

Relationship advisor Dexter Bryant is trying to shake his stud-for-hire image, but when Asia Carpenter makes him an offer he can't refuse, Dex will have to play the role of professional rebound guy one last time.

Romances from Harlequin Kimani!

The New York Sabers

*Don't miss my sizzling **New York Sabers** football series! Check my website for details!*

Bayou Dreams

Check out my brand new series set in the small, fictional town of Gauthier, Louisiana!

About the Author:

USA Today Bestselling author Farrah Rochon hails from a small town just west of New Orleans. She has garnered much acclaim for her Holmes Brothers, New York Sabers, Bayou Dreams and Moments in Maplesville series. *I'll Catch You*, the second book in her New York Sabers series for Harlequin Kimani, was a 2012 RITA ® Award finalist. Yours Forever, the third book in the Bayou Dreams series, was a 2015 RITA® Award finalist. Farrah has been nominated for an RT BOOKReviews Reviewers Choice Award, and in 2015 received the Emma Award for Author of the Year.

When she is not writing in her favorite coffee shop, Farrah spends most of her time reading her favorite romance novels or seeing as many Broadway shows as possible. An admitted sports fanatic, Farrah feeds her addiction to football by watching New Orleans Saints games on Sunday afternoons.